A
Harlequin
Romance

OTHER
Harlequin Romances
by MARGARET MALCOLM

DEAR TYRANT

by

MARGARET MALCOLM

HARLEQUIN BOOKS   TORONTO
WINNIPEG

Original hard cover edition published in 1953
by Mills & Boon Limited under the title "Beloved Tyrant".

This edition © Margaret Malcolm 1975

SBN 373-01864-9

Harlequin edition published March 1975

The Harlequin trade mark, consisting of the word
HARLEQUIN and the portrayal of a Harlequin, is registered
in the United States Patent Office and in the Canada Trade
Marks Office.

Printed in Canada

CHAPTER ONE

THE MAN sitting on the terrace in the clear, bright sunshine looked so out of the picture that more than one passer-by spared him a second glance.

His well-cut tweeds contrasted sharply with their ski-ing suits or the short skirts of the girls who were or had been skating, but that was not what caught their attention. Far greater than the contrast between their clothes and his was his obvious difference of mood. Theirs was the light-hearted mood of a holiday. Fergus Imray's was very definitely not.

It was not that he was incapable of joining them and more than likely teaching them something at their own game, but this time he had not come to Switzerland for the sports. He had come on business. And it was business that he did not relish. He had arrived at the hotel, famous both for its luxury and the beauty of its surroundings, less than half an hour ago, but in that time he had come to the conclusion that his task was going to be extremely difficult and distasteful.

Typically, Fergus had come to the conclusion that since it was distasteful, the only thing to do was to get it over quickly. But that turned out to be impossible.

As soon as he had registered, even before he had seen his room, he had asked the clerk on the inquiry desk to find Vicky Pallant for him.

The man smiled at him pityingly.

"But Miss Pallant is out," he explained. "She is one of a bobsleigh crew. And there is a contest today. That is why there are so few people about."

"I see," Fergus said, his fair, heavy brows almost meeting in a frown. "In that case, I shall be glad if you will send her a message telling her that I am here and asking her to come back at once."

"But —" the man began and stopped, shrugging his shoulders. He had met Fergus's type before. Men

5

with whom it was impossible to argue because they were so sure of themselves. None the less, he had a soft spot for Vicky and he would do his best. "I do not think you quite understand, monsieur. If mademoiselle comes back to the hotel before the contest is concluded, her crew is disqualified. She is the captain, you see."

"Quite," Fergus said curtly. "None the less, it is imperative that Miss Pallant should come and see me at once. I must repeat, I shall be glad if you will send a messenger to her — immediately!"

Again the shrug. What was the use? All too well, the clerk knew that men like Fergus frequently have some sort of influence with the management — and he had no wish to lose his job.

"Certainly, monsieur." Punctiliously, he wrote out the message and solemnly gave orders for its dispatch. But inwardly, he was grinning. This Englishman — no, probably Scotsman — with his grim mouth and his air of command might give all the orders he liked, but nothing was more unlikely than that the little Pallant girl would come back to the hotel one single second before she wished.

And that, Fergus discovered when the messenger returned, was the case.

"Mademoiselle sent her regrets," the man said, obviously clothing Vicky's careless message with the gloss of formality. "She cannot come at present. She asks monsieur to meet her in the American bar at half-past six."

"I see," Fergus said shortly.

And he did see. Very clearly. Even Vicky's father had spoken of her as a handful, though, admittedly, there had been genuine admiration in his voice at the time. Fergus felt no such admiration. As far as he was concerned, she was a spoilt, troublesome child who stood in need of a good smacking. She had done for years. And now, fate was going to deliver her a tremendous blow and he, Fergus, was to be the instrument which delivered it.

Well, there was nothing for it but to wait until

Vicky chose to turn up. He was reasonably sure that his message had not been delivered with any degree of urgency, but, to be fair to the man, he did not think it would have made much difference if it had. Obstinacy was another of Vicky's traits.

None the less, he saw her before the time that she had appointed for their meeting. Tiring, after a while, of the very perfection of the scene before his eyes, he came into the lounge and settled himself in a quiet corner of it, almost hidden by a large and ornate pillar.

Vicky drifted in, one of a laughing, chattering crowd. He recognised some of her companions. There was Lance Ingleton and his sister, Glenda. Officially, their mother was supposed to be the chaperone for the group of youngsters who made up the greater proportion of the party but, if Fergus knew anything about Mrs. Ingleton — and he knew a lot more than that lady would wish — she took her duties very lightly. There were the Corwell twins and Becky and Dick Hanyon, a young married couple. There were four or five other people whom he did not know, but he could recognise one thing that they had in common with the rest. All of them were used to having plenty of money to spend. As Vicky was.

He concluded that Vicky's crew must have won, for her voice was high and rather shrill with excitement. Yes, evidently she had steered them to victory. They were toasting her, and Vicky's face was glowing with something more than the sting of the fresh air from which she had just come. He had to admit that he had never seen her looking so attractive. Her scarlet suit that might have looked garish on the wrong girl was exactly right for her with her pale, clear skin and her smooth black head of hair. Even now, he thought, when other girls' hair looked ruffled and in need of attention, Vicky's still looked like a sleek, black satin cap. For some reason her perfection irritated him. But the next moment his irritation was directed against himself for having let anything

7

to do with her influence him one way or another
He was here on business — he must not forget that

For a moment he deliberated on the possibility of
cutting her out from the crowd and telling her what
he had to at once. But it would not be easy. There
would be a fuss — quite likely, she would insist on
his joining them, and that he had no intention of
doing. In his profession, he knew quite a lot about
his clients and their friends, and he had no liking
for Vicky's set.

No, he would keep his appointment with her at
the time she had suggested.

She was ten minutes late. She had not meant to
be, but it had been such fun to linger in the hot bath
and gloat over the success of the day. And then,
somehow, fancy dress always took longer to get into
than ordinary clothes. It was going to be fun, this
ball! Particularly as she knew that she would look
her best, though her costume was not particularly
original. She was a columbine. Her long, slim legs
were encased in sheerest nylon, her white and silver
skirts bunched out round her slim hips like rose
petals and her bodice sparkled with silver sequins.
There was a sequin-sewn cap on her smooth, dark
head.

Her reflection in the mirrors that lined the great
staircase was so satisfactory that, as she ran down
to meet Fergus, her high spirits bubbled over despite
his dour appearance.

"Utterly honest," she remembered her father had
said of him. "And utterly without humour or a spice
of adventure! Just as well in a solicitor, no doubt.
But — grim in a pal!"

"Hallo!" she greeted him. "I'm sorry I'm late, but
it was worth the effort, don't you think?" She re-
volved slowly in front of him.

"Charming," Fergus said mechanically, and Vicky
grimaced. Still, one had to be sorry for people who
got so little out of life! She would try to see that
he had a good time tonight — it would be difficult
not to, Vicky thought joyfully.

8

She wriggled up on to one of the high stools at the bar, and beamed at him.

"One wants good legs for an outfit like this," she confided. "And —" she stretched hers out for his inspection, "you can't say I haven't got them!"

He glanced down, but it was at her shoes rather than her slender legs. She was wearing little silver pumps with cross-over ribbons, like a child's. They made him think of the dancing lessons to which he, an unwilling small boy, had been dragged. The little girls had worn just such shoes — and not much smaller, either. It made him remember just how young this girl was — eighteen — nineteen? Little more than a child herself.

"What did you want to see me about?" Vicky asked cheerfully. "I'm sorry that I couldn't come in earlier, by the way, but it really was impossible. You can't let your crew down, you know."

Fergus did not answer immediately, and suddenly his silence seemed ominous to Vicky. She looked up into his lean, harshly delineated face and for the first time saw that there was something more in his gravity than just an habitual expression.

She slipped off her perch and unconsciously gripped his wrist.

"It's bad news, isn't it?" she asked, and when he nodded, she led the way quickly to a deserted conservatory.

"Go on," she commanded, standing very straight and erect so that he should not know how she was trembling. "It's — something about Daddy, isn't it?"

"Yes." He hesitated, and she could have screamed at him to go on — not to leave her in this agonising uncertainty. "I'm afraid there isn't any way in which I can break this gently to you, Vicky. There has been- an accident —"

"You mean — he's dead, don't you?" Vicky asked stonily. And when he nodded, she walked slowly over to the other side of the conservatory so that her back was towards him.

"It had to happen some day." She was surprised

that she could speak so steadily, but she could not let go — not in front of this grim man. "Daddy loved taking risks. So do I. So I understand. Was it — quick?"

"Very quick," he assured her.

There was a long silence and then, without moving, Vicky heard herself saying, gruffly:

"It was decent of you to come out and tell me. You can't have liked the job."

"I thought it would be better for you to have someone with whom to travel on your way home," he explained matter-of-factly.

"On my way home?" She turned slowly and her small white face, torn though it was with emotion, was very resolute. Slowly she shook her head. "I don't suppose you will understand this, Mr. Imray, but — I don't think I shall come home. Not yet. Not until I have got used to — this. You see, Father *was* home. Now — it doesn't much matter where I am. Besides, he did so want me to have this holiday. I know, as well as if he were here to tell me so, that he would want me to complete it. Oh, I know people will say things — you don't approve, I can see. But — Daddy and I knew one another so well. He'd tell me to — to keep my chin up and — carry on."

Her voice broke and there were tears in her grey eyes. Silently Fergus cursed the dead man whom this child had so idolised — with so little cause.

"I'm afraid that will not be possible," he said grimly.

"Not? But why? You mean, it isn't conventional? But then, we never have been, Daddy and I —"

"That was not what I had in mind," he said slowly. "Vicky, what financial arrangements did your father make for you?"

"Financial arrangements?" She shook her head. "None. At least, I mean, I didn't have an allowance. I just spent the money he gave me and then I went to him for more."

"I see. And have you much at the moment?" he inquired.

She shook her head.

"Not very much. I was going to write to him and ask if he could wangle something — Oh, I see what you are worrying about!" There was a note of scorn in her voice. "It takes time to get things sorted out, doesn't it? Well, surely you can lend me some and I can pay you back by and by —"

But now it was his turn to shake his head.

"No, Vicky, you can't do that."

"I'm sure it could be arranged —" she began, but he stopped her.

"Vicky, I'm sorry, but you have got to know. There isn't any money out of which you could repay me. Your father was — bankrupt."

Childlishly she clapped her hands over her mouth to hold back the scream that rose to her lips.

"Oh, no, no! That can't be right. There has always been money — you must be wrong —"

"I wish I were," he said emphatically. "But there is no mistake. It is true, there is some money, but when all the debts are paid —"

"There is the house —" she said eagerly. "Daddy paid twenty thousand pounds for it —"

"That will have to go as well," he told her quietly.

And at last she understood.

"You mean — more than that?"

He could have told her it was infinitely more than that. That Mark Pallant had indeed, as she had said, enjoyed taking risks. He was a born gambler with an infallible gift for using chance as if it were certainty. It seemed as if he could not make a mistake. Until one day his luck turned, as it always would with men like Mark. And he had not been able to believe it. He continued gambling, as he had always done, taking greater and still greater risks in order to pull his affairs off the rocks, until there had come a day when he had known that it was hopeless.

Suddenly Vicky broke down. She was frightened,

really frightened. "What shall I do?" she whispered to herself rather than to Fergus. "What can I do?" And her face crumpled up like a child's.

Fergus looked at her thoughtfully. It was the question that he had asked himself many times. There were quite a few young men in her set, but he had not heard of any probable engagement and, in any case, this news would certainly put an end to any possibility of such a thing. They were nothing if not practical, these amusement-loving people.

"Have you no relations?" he suggested, but she shook her head.

"Mother and — Father were both only children. There isn't anybody —"

Strive as she would, she could not restrain the rising note of panic in her voice.

"In that case, you will have to find work —"

Vicky gasped. His suggestion chilled and startled her as if he had thrown cold water over her and, resentfully, she knew that he had done it quite deliberately, sensing her panic.

"There must be something that you can do which will enable you to earn your living?" he went on.

Vicky pulled herself together. She was furious that she had let this cold, unsympathetic man see into her mind. He didn't understand that, even if you did your best not to make a fuss, you could be just chewed up inside —

"I expect so — if I have to," she said casually.

"You will have to," he told her inflexibly. "You must make up your mind to that. Have you passed any examinations?"

"At school, you mean?" she asked, and involuntarily a ghost of a smile flickered over her face. "I never even got so far as them suggesting that I should sit for an exam! I'm not very clever, you see."

"That is a pity," he said gravely. "It closes so many avenues to you. But there must be something that you can do?"

She shook her head.

"I can dance — rather well. But not well enough

to be a professional. I can sing a bit — paint a little —" her voice trailed away inconclusively before his disapproving expression.

"That makes it very difficult," he admitted. Then he went on slowly. "Of course, there is always one job that is open to you. One for which there are never enough applicants and for which you will need no more than an ordinary standard of intelligence."

"That sounds like me," Vicky said wanly. "Go on, I'll buy it!"

"You could be a companion to an invalid or to an elderly person," he went on.

"Oh, no!" she said quickly.

"Can you suggest anything else?" he asked.

"I — I don't know yet," she stammered. "But — I have friends —"

"They are what you want at a time like this," he said slowly, and Vicky looked at him quickly.

"You don't think that they will stand by me, now that there isn't any money, do you?"

Fergus shook his head.

"You are reading something into my words that I certainly did not mean to imply," he said gravely. "Yet — if you will have it, it *is* a test of friendship."

"Yes, and my friends will stand up to the test!" she predicted defiantly. "Just you wait and see!"

"Very well, we will leave it at that for the moment," he agreed, his eyes resting thoughtfully on her pretty, tawdry finery. "But — if you should find that, after all, you are interested, I can offer you a position such as I suggested myself."

"Oh?" Vicky said very softly. "Could you, Mr. Imray? Perhaps you had better tell me something about it?"

"My mother is a semi-invalid," he replied. "She has an elderly maid who looks after her, but she needs someone who can give her a different type of companionship from anything Maggie is capable of. She needs someone to help her with her correspondence, to read to her and to encourage her to go out a little. And so on."

"But," Vicky said speculatively, "supposing you engaged me and your mother did not approve of the arrangement?"

"She would," Fergus said positively. "She always approves of what I do."

"How very nice for you!" Vicky said gently. "And — how much would you pay me, Mr. Imray?"

Fergus studied her grave little face closely. He did not know her sufficiently well to read her mind from each fresh inflection of her voice, but instinct told him that there was danger ahead.

"I have already interviewed several people, none of whom was satisfactory," and he told her what they had been asking.

Vicky mused, "Do you know, Mr. Imray, at that rate the watch I am wearing would cost a year's salary?"

He glanced down at the pretty thing and nodded.

"I should say that it was a fair price," he said consideringly.

And then Vicky's self-control snapped. She had tried to be brave, tried to keep her chin up, but now she could bear no more. And because she would not let him see her grief, she let him see her temper instead.

"And you dare — you *dare* offer me a job like that!" she gasped furiously. "Father said that you always counted your ha'pence and now I know that he was right! You thought that I should be so desperate that you could underpay me for doing a job that you can't get anyone else to take on! Oh, if I could make you understand how I despise you — I'd rather beg in the gutter than work for you —"

"Well, fortunately, you have no intention of taking the job, so why discuss it?" he asked equably. "I shall be staying here until tomorrow. If I can be of any service to you, please call on me. If not, you will be receiving a statement of the exact position of your father's affairs as soon as we have gone thoroughly into them. Might I suggest that you should find your friends now and —"

"Vicky — I say, Vicky, I've been hunting everywhere for you!" Glenda Ingleton, dressed as a shepherdess, came hurrying into the conservatory. She was holding a newspaper in her hand and involuntarily Fergus made a movement as if to take it from her. But it was too late.

"Something awful has happened!" Glenda blurted out. "It's in the English paper. Vicky, your father — he's committed suicide!"

Vicky did not speak, but her hand flew to her throat as if she were choking, and her wide, horrified eyes sought Fergus's. She gazed imploringly up into his face and slowly he bent his head.

Vicky gave a soft little moan, and Fergus was just in time to catch her up in his arms as she fainted.

"You little fool!" he said bitterly to the contrite Glenda. "She could at least have been spared that!"

A light pierced the black world in which Vicky had been wandering, and by it she saw the faces of the people who were bending over her. Mrs. Ingleton, a chambermaid and a scared-looking Glenda. Her eyes wandered beyond them, but there was no sign of Fergus Imray.

"Drink this, mademoiselle — yes, every drop. It will do you good — help me, madame, to lift her, if you please."

Obediently, because it was too much trouble to refuse, Vicky sipped down the *sal volatile*, and gradually the mists cleared. But memory returned as well, and Vicky closed her eyes as if to shut it out.

"She will be all right now," she heard Mrs. Ingleton say. "Thank you, Elise, you have been most helpful."

There was a chink of money, a soft: "Thank you, madame!" and the sound of the door being quietly shut.

"Now, Glenda, run down to Mr. Imray and tell him that there is nothing to worry about. Vicky is quite all right now!"

"Yes, mother," Glenda said obediently.

Vicky did not open her eyes. More than anything else in the world, she wanted to be alone, quite, quite alone until she had had time to hide her hurt from curious or even sympathetic eyes. But it was impossible to ask Mrs. Ingleton to go, which that lady showed no signs of doing. Instead, she sat down beside the bed on which they had laid Vicky, and said kindly but firmly:

"Now, Vicky, we are going to have a talk about this! Oh, I know, you would like me to go away, but someone has got to help you pull yourself together, and there appears to be no one but me. Please do your best to be sensible, Vicky, for it is neither an easy nor a pleasant task for me to undertake!"

Vicky sat up suddenly.

"Then, please, can't we just leave things — for a little while," she suggested. "I — really will try not to make a fuss but —" her face began to work, and Mrs. Ingleton sighed resignedly.

"My dear Vicky, I am a good many years older than you are and a good deal more experienced. Believe me, the idea that you will feel better after a good cry is quite wrong. Make an effort right from the beginning to control yourself and you will find it is increasingly easy! That sounds very hard, I know, but I am speaking for your own good."

Vicky did not reply, and after a moment Mrs. Ingleton went on:

"I suppose Fergus Imray came over to tell you about this unfortunate business."

"Yes," Vicky said briefly.

"So you already knew when Glenda — I can't see why you fainted at all!" Mrs. Ingleton's high-pitched voice was faintly querulous. "You had had time to get over the first shock —"

"No," Vicky said, low-voiced. "Mr. Imray had told me that there had been an accident —"

"Odd!" Mrs. Ingleton commented. "I've never known him reluctant to pass on unpleasant news before. One of those relentless men who call a spade a spade no matter what the circumstances.

Yes, perhaps it was strange, Vicky agreed silently. And then dismissed the thought, because close on its heels came another. Surely it was even stranger that her best friend, unlike the man to whom she was absolutely nothing, had been so careless of her feelings —

"But I really can't make out why — I mean Mark, of all men —"

"Daddy had lost all his money," Vicky said mechanically, and Mrs. Ingleton gave a little gasp.

"Lost all his money!" she said shrilly. "Oh, there must be some mistake! I mean — that sort of thing can't happen in five minutes, and your father never showed a sign —" She stopped abruptly, suddenly realising that, after all, that was not so surprising. People like Mark who gambled their way through life could never afford to show if they were down on their luck. "Did Mr. Imray say how bad things were?"

"He said that there would be no money and that the house would have to go —" Vicky said wearily. Her head was throbbing violently now, and Mrs. Ingleton's none too tactful probing was like a brilliant light turned on her shrinking heart.

Mrs. Ingleton clicked her tongue expressively.

"As bad as that!" she said disapprovingly. "I really can't think what Mark — but, Vicky, I always understood that you had money of your own — some that your mother had left to you —"

Of course she had! Ever so little, Vicky's spirits lifted. Then she remembered that Mr. Imray had always looked after her affairs as well as her father's. He knew that she had at least some money from that source. And yet, he had told her that there was nothing. That she would have to work. Did that mean all that had gone too?

"Of course," she heard Mrs. Ingleton say thoughtfully, "your mother made your father your guardian and trustee. That may have gone with the rest. Probably has, I should imagine!"

She stood up and for a moment looked down at Vicky. There was a certain amount of sympathy in her expression, because Viola Ingleton had a very shrewd appreciation of the value of money and quite genuinely pitied anyone who hadn't got it. None the less, as the mother of a son, her paramount feeling was one of relief that this had happened now and not in a few months' time. It was not that she had thought there was anything between Lance and Vicky or, for that matter, between Vicky and anyone else. Vicky was having too good a time to want to settle down. But all the same, one never knew what might not develop with these young people, and Lance had got to look facts fairly in the face. He was a dear boy, but he would never make a place for himself in the world, and though his father could and would continue to make him a good allowance, it really was necessary for him to marry money. How terrible it would have been had there been anything between him and Vicky and then this had happened! Yes, she certainly had cause for gratitude.

"Well, my dear, I expect you would like to have a little rest," Mrs. Ingleton suggested briskly. "I will arrange for you to have dinner up in your own room, for I don't suppose you will want to come down tonight. Indeed it would be rather —" her voice trailed away inconclusively under the direct gaze of Vicky's grey eyes.

"Rather inconsiderate of me," Vicky supplied in a hard little voice. You need not worry, Mrs. Ingleton, I shall be very sensible and — and practical —"

"You really are a very good little girl, Vicky," Mrs. Ingleton brushed Vicky's forehead with her lips, reading more, perhaps, into what Vicky had said than was perhaps really there.

And then, to Vicky's relief, she went. Instantly, Vicky slipped off the bed and began tearing at the columbine dress. The first crisp freshness of it had gone, crushed on the bed on which she had been

18

lying, and as Vicky tossed it carelessly into a corner, it sank down into a little heap like the dejected ghost of her own happiness.

She put on a dark dressing-gown and sat down in front of her dressing-table. Involuntarily her eyes met those of her reflection, and it seemed to Vicky that she was looking at the face of a stranger. Somebody much older than she was, somebody whose face was pinched and white and whose mouth drooped at the corners, whose eyes were haunted —

Suddenly she buried her face in her folded arms. She *was* haunted — she always would be — by the knowledge that the person she had loved best in the world, whom she had believed loved her beyond everything else, had failed her. What did it matter about the money! They could have started life again somewhere, somehow, and they would have made out! But instead of that, her father had not had the courage to face up to things as he had always taught her to do. And worse than that, he had left her to face up to them alone.

That was what hurt so hideously. He had put on her slender shoulders a burden that he hadn't had the courage to bear himself. And in doing so, he had severed the tie between himself and Vicky as death alone could never have done.

She could not put it as clearly as that to herself, but deep within her was the longing for reassurance from someone she could trust. She had spoken so proudly of her friends, and now they had left her quite alone as if she were an outcast —

There was a light tap on her door and Glenda came in. She was a pretty, shallow little thing whose emotions went no deeper than a butterfly's. She had just experienced a none too pleasant ten minutes with her mother for her part in the sad little drama, and consequently she was all contrition.

"Vicky, I *am* sorry," she said earnestly. "I was a silly little fool — just like Mr. Imray said."

"He had no right —" Vicky began, and stopped. After all, what did it matter? "Don't worry, Glenda," she went on gently. "I expect you were so shocked you didn't realise —"

"That was it," Glenda agreed eagerly. "You know the way, when things startle you, they just sort of burst out —"

Vicky thought desperately:

"I wanted someone to come, but now, I wish she would go! I don't want to be pitied —"

Glenda rattled on:

"Everybody is so sorry, Vicky. They asked me to say so. Lance and some of the other boys wanted to send you some flowers, but Mother stopped them."

Vicky looked at her sharply.

"Your mother — but why?"

Glenda twisted her fingers nervously.

"Oh — well, you know what Mother is like! Awfully practical. She's been giving Lance a terrific talking to —"

"But what for?" Vicky asked.

"Well — you know, he hasn't got any money of his own, and so — well, Mummy keeps on saying she does not want him to marry for money but he can't marry where it isn't?"

"But —" Vicky looked really startled. "There isn't anything — I mean Lance and I don't feel in the least —"

"That's what Lance and I kept on telling her, but she had got it into her head and we can't get it out." Glenda gazed at her with wide blue eyes that were filled with avid curiosity. "What are you going to do, Vicky?"

Vicky's hands, dug deep into the pockets of her housecoat, were clenched so tightly that the nails were cutting into her palms.

"I haven't quite made up my mind yet," she said in a steady, controlled voice. "You see, it has all been so sudden —" she bit her lip with small, even teeth.

"Darling, of course," Glenda said, all contrition again. "I think you are being absolutely wonderful —

what I'd do if I were in your place I simply don't know —"

Suddenly Vicky interrupted her.

"Glenda, do you mind very much leaving me alone now? I've got a lot to think of and — and you don't want to miss any of the ball, do you? I can hear the band tuning up!"

Glenda gave a little scream.

"Oh, I must fly!" She gave Vicky a hug. "Tomorrow morning I'll come along and we'll talk everything over! I'm sure Daddy will find you something —"

She fluttered away, and at last Vicky was alone again.

She stood very still in the middle of the beautiful room for which she had no longer any money to pay, and knew that, quite unconsciously, Glenda had made it very clear to her just how people would regard her now. An outcast, a person who needed charity, who was no longer their equal. And yet, had she learned anything that she had not already known in her heart of hearts?

She had told Fergus Imray that she could trust her friends to stand up to the test of her altered fortunes, but she knew that she had said it all the more loudly because of that hideous, lurking fear.

The fear that there was nobody in the whole world that one could trust. Not even one's best friends —

In another hour, Fergus would be leaving for the airport. Since he had handed Vicky over to the care of Mrs. Ingleton, he had not set eyes on her again. He had inquired of that lady how she was and Mrs. Ingleton had assured him that Vicky was quite all right.

"Upset, of course," she said, and added with the optimism that such natures always reserve for the troubles of others, "But she is young. She will get over it."

"Naturally," Fergus said dryly. "Especially with such good friends around her."

Mrs. Ingleton had looked at him sharply and de-

21

cided, not for the first time, that she did not like this fair-haired man whose dark eyes had such a gimlet-like quality.

Fergus had, of course, been fully aware of her feelings, but they left him completely untroubled. A man given to ploughing a straight furrow regardless of the opinion of others, he was not likely to be diverted from it by anyone for whom he had so little liking as Mrs. Ingleton.

He glanced down frowningly at his watch. He had sent a note along to Vicky's room that morning telling her just when he was leaving and again placing himself at her disposal, but so far there had been no sign from her that she wished to see him again. Frankly, he was not surprised. After all, what was there for her to say?

Not for the first time, he found himself wondering what would happen to this pretty, spoilt child. True, it was no concern of his, but then it did not seem to be the concern of anyone. He had surprised himself with that offer of a job, and even as he had spoken of it, he had realised the futility of trying to make her understand just how serious her position was. Well, he had received what no doubt Vicky felt to be a well-deserved snub, and now there was nothing more that he could do.

Really, he might as well start now for all the good that waiting would do, and yet he knew quite well that he would wait punctiliously until the exact moment that he had told her he would leave.

And suddenly the telephone bell rang. He lifted the receiver. Unlikely that it was Vicky as late as this —

"Fergus Imray speaking," he said impersonally.

"This is Vicky Pallant," the quiet voice was equally impersonal. "Mr. Imray, if the offer of the job which you made me last night is still open I should like to accept it!"

CHAPTER TWO

IF VICKY had startled Fergus Imray with her announcement, she could hear no indication of it as he said coolly:

"Very well, Vicky. Can you be ready to leave in half an hour? I have not cancelled the reservation I had made for you, so there will be no difficulty about it."

Vicky clenched the hand that lay in her lap. He had been so sure that he knew just what would happen and what she would do as a result. She would have given all she had to have been able to tell him that he had been just too clever because she was staying on as the guest of her friends until the end of her holiday, but — no one had felt like making such an offer. Not a soul had come near her the whole evening, and while they danced to the gay strains of the band that Vicky could hear in her room, she was left utterly alone.

"I am ready now," she told him. "Everything is packed. I shall have two small cases with me, the rest can come on after."

"Good!" He took her preparedness just as calmly as he had the announcement that she had changed her mind. Probably, she thought, the only thing that struck him as strange was that she had left it as late as this before getting in touch with him. But, foolishly, up to the very last moment, she had hoped that something would happen — though just what, she would have found it difficult to say.

But nothing had happened, and now it was too late. She had burned her boats and now all she wanted was to get away as fast as possible.

"There is one thing —" and for the first time she could not check a falter in her voice. "My account here. Can you — will you settle it and then, when we get back to England, I will find some way to pay you — sell some of my jewellery —"

"Yes, I will see to that," he promised. "Meet me in the vestibule in a quarter of an hour's time. And Vicky —"

"Yes?" she asked rather breathlessly.

"Be sure that you have your passport and any other papers easily accessible," he told her.

"Yes, of course," she said mechanically. But that, she was sure, was not what he had intended saying. Just for one foolish second she had thought that he was going to say something human and kind and re-assuring, but of course, she had been mistaken. After all, why should he? And why should she want him to? Theirs was a purely business relationship, and that was the way it had better remain.

Just for a moment, when she was quite ready to go down to join him, Vicky stood in front of the glass that had reflected her image so many times — before which she had prinked only last night in the columbine costume that was now thrust carelessly into the bottom of one of her trunks.

The girl who looked into the mirror now was a very different person. She had lost all her gaiety and sparkle, and in its place was a deliberate, studied composure that Vicky intended to be a barrier be-tween her old and her new self.

For during the long, restless night she had had plenty of time to think things out, and she had come to the conclusion that there was only one thing for her to do. She must shut the door on the past as if it had never existed. And, in a way, it never had except in her imagination. Thoughtlessly, in her youth-ful exuberance, she had taken it for granted that the world was a wonderful place and that people were decent and kind and good. Now she knew that they were nothing of the sort. That the very people on whom you had the right to expect you could rely were idols with feet of clay.

Vicky was too young and too inexperienced to be aware of anything but the blackest of blacks and the whitest of whites in life. A thing was right or it was wrong. Good or bad. There was no half-way for

Vicky. So now, her world had crashed and there was no chance whatever that it could ever be rebuilt. Very well, then, she would not try to. She would accept the world as she now knew it really was. Hard and cruel and just waiting to do one an injury. She would not shut her eyes or try to bargain with it, and then she would be safe because, expecting neither generosity nor kindness, she need not be afraid of being hurt.

That was why she was going to work for Fergus Imray. She would be perfectly safe with him, because she understood so exactly how his mind worked. He had seen an opportunity of getting someone to look after his mother — he had admitted that it had not been an easy thing to do — and he had taken it. Vicky, on the other hand, realised that she must have time to look about her and find something more congenial to do. It was quite impossible for her to stay on in Switzerland, and as the house that had been her home was to be sold she must have somewhere to live in the meantime. If Fergus considered the arrangement a permanent one while she regarded it as merely temporary, that was his look-out. After all, if she were not satisfactory, he could easily dismiss her. But she would be satisfactory. She would see to that. Her small, scarlet mouth set in a thin, resolute line. She was not going to give him the satisfaction of pulling her up for some fault if she could help it.

She glanced down at her watch, the same diamond-encrusted one that she had thrust out for Fergus's inspection the night before, and gave a little gasp. This was it — zero hour!

She picked up her two cases and took the lift down to the ground floor. Fergus was waiting for her, and he took the cases from her.

"You should have had them brought down for you," he told her, but Vicky shook her head.

"I hadn't enough money to tip him," she explained composedly. "You see, I told you, I hadn't much."

"What would you have done —" he began, and

25

she raised her dark brows and finished the sentence for him.

"If this had not happened? Borrowed, of course. People never mind lending money to you when it isn't awfully important. It is only when you need it desperately that they start getting careful."

Despite her rigid control, her voice quivered ever so slightly, but Fergus did not appear to notice, for he simply nodded and commented:

"A very useful lesson to have learnt! Now, if you are ready —"

There was a car waiting for them, and without a backward glance, Vicky got into it. Automatically she took the farther seat so that Fergus could get in without needing to pass her. Resolutely, she stared straight ahead, permitting herself to see neither the curious faces of acquaintances already setting off for the day's sport, nor the beauty of their surroundings.

One or two people raised their hands in a tentative sort of farewell gesture, but Vicky did not respond. Better to make a complete break from the world to which she no longer belonged and where she was no longer wanted.

To her relief, when they reached the airport, Fergus did not attempt to make conversation. From a small case he produced a book which, judging from the position of the marker, he had been reading on his outward journey and, in addition, a couple of magazines which he handed to Vicky with the comment that he hoped she had not seen them already.

"Thank you," she said mechanically. "No, I haven't seen them."

She could have added that she had not had time for reading at all during her holiday. Every moment of the day had been taken up with ski-ing and bob-sleighing, and every evening, far into the night, she had danced . . .

When all the formalities were completed they had little more than a quarter of an hour to wait before, over the loud-speaker system, they were summoned to their waiting 'plane.

It seemed to Vicky, as she was checked into the 'plane, that her name was positively shouted, and it was certainly true that several people turned their heads quickly to look at her. She stumbled a little, and instantly Fergus's hand was under her elbow.

"Steady, Vicky!" he said quietly, and her head went up. Why couldn't he be like other people who rarely guessed what was going on inside one's head instead of being able to look into it as if through a window? He had known perfectly well that she had stumbled because she had suddenly realised just how much publicity had been given to her father's death, and had shrunk away from it. Evidently she, too, had some news value.

She sat down on her seat and then, with Fergus beside her, she found to her relief that she was shut away from curious eyes. She rested her head wearily against the high back of the seat and closed her eyes, but almost immediately Fergus said:

"Do up your safety-belt, Vicky!" and mechanically she obeyed.

The engines came to life, the chocks were removed, and the plane taxied to its runway. A few minutes later they were airborne.

And from the small window beside her, Vicky said good-bye to Switzerland. The sun was shining, and it made the snow completely dazzling in its purity. They passed over clustered villages, the roofs of the houses covered with a blanket of snow, over the hotel where Vicky had been staying and even over the run where she had triumphed only yesterday — although it seemed years ago now.

Vicky's eyes dropped to the magazines that Fergus had provided for her, and she began to turn the pages mechanically. She had not the least idea what was on them, but at least to gaze down at them kept her from looking out of the window at the beautiful land so quickly vanishing behind them as her own happiness had vanished.

And then, as they got nearer to England, there was no view at all. Thick swirling mist cut them off in a world of their own, and when they came down at London Airport it was to find a typically drab November day awaiting them.

In spite of her fur coat and fur-lined boots, Vicky found that she was shivering. Evidently Fergus noticed it, for he glanced down at his watch and said briskly:

"I have ordered a car to take us straight up to Euston, but there is time to have a cup of coffee first."

"It doesn't matter," Vicky said quickly, but found that he had apparently not heard her.

It took Vicky longer to get through the Customs than it did Fergus, for details had to be given of the luggage that was still to come, but at last they were both through and the hired car turned out on to the dark, greasy road.

It was from then on that the journey seemed a nightmare to Vicky. Somehow, both car and train seemed so incredibly slow. In congenial company and different circumstances it would not have mattered, but as it was, the dreary monotony seemed unending, and Fergus Imray's grim silence — seemingly so much more oppressive in the restricted space of a car and then of the compartment that they had to themselves — pressed like a weight on her spirits.

It was not that she wanted him to talk or that she would have been able to reply if he did. They were not, she thought, the sort of people who could ever be friends. It was true that he looked after her in an impersonal if competent manner, but only once did he show himself at all human.

After dinner, when they had returned to their compartment he suddenly leaned forward and said thoughtfully:

"Vicky, I want to tell you a little bit about my mother."

Instantly, she sat erect. Until now, it had been a queer, nebulous relationship that had existed between them on the journey. He had not exactly been in charge of her, although he had assumed all the responsibilities of it as a man naturally would. Nor had his attitude been exactly that of an employer. But now, with the distance to his home and the time when she assumed her duties decreasing with every moment, evidently he felt the necessity of getting the situation into its proper perspective.

"Yes, Mr. Imray?" In spite of the fact that she was very, very tired, there was a brisk alertness in her tone.

He hesitated for a moment and then began slowly:

"My mother is little and frail and very brave. She needs to be. She is practically a cripple with arthritis, and she knows that there is no cure for it. Sometimes she finds things a little easier, but in general —" he shook his head, and his face was very bitter. "If you have ever had to stand by and see someone you care for suffer and know that all your money cannot help them, you will understand how I feel."

Vicky looked at him in astonishment. He was the last man whom she had ever expected to hear speak with such feeling, and the strange thing was that it did not occur to her to doubt the genuineness of his affection for his mother. She found it impossible to reply, and Fergus, with a subtle change of tone, went on:

"That is why I am giving you fair warning now, Vicky, that I will stand no slackness or lack of interest and kindness from you. You are under the impression that I offered you this job because I could get your services cheap. You were never more wrong. I would willingly pay twice that if I could find someone who would help to make her days a little more endurable. In fact, if you succeed in doing that, I shall willingly pay you more —"

"Thank you, Mr. Imray, but I am quite content with what you suggested last night," Vicky said stiffly. "I agreed to come for that, and I will stick to my side of the bargain!"

"I intend to see to it that you do!" he retorted, and Vicky's pale face flushed.

"Can't you ever credit people with decent feelings

— or honesty —" she began hotly, and stopped. Why should he? She didn't any more — it only seemed it was not always possible to remember that.

"Yes, I can," Fergus admitted, apparently not having recognised why she had broken off her sentence in the middle. "When I've proved to my own satisfaction that such is the case. But I've got beyond the age when one takes decency for granted. You will be wise too, Vicky, to remember that."

"Yes, Mr. Imray," Vicky said so meekly that Fergus looked at her sharply. He, like Vicky herself, had realised that she was a very different person from the girl he had gone to see. That girl, if she had spoken with such disarming meekness, would, undoubtedly, have had her tongue in her cheek. But this Vicky — he did not know. And his inability even to guess added just one more complication to an already sufficiently complex situation.

Nor did it afford him any satisfaction to know that, to a large extent, he had created the situation through his own actions. He could have said, with complete accuracy, that he was not a man whose life was governed by impulses, and yet now he had indulged in one the results of which were impossible to calculate.

And yet, what else could he have done? Spoilt and irresponsible she might be, but her father's death — especially the manner of it — had undoubtedly been a terrible blow. Now, if ever, she needed someone to stand by her, and the only person had been himself. Well, he had done his best and if, in the doing of it, he had been somewhat reluctant, few people would blame him for that. What was so grimly humorous was that Vicky imputed such totally different motives to his offer. She had thought that he had seen an opportunity for striking a shrewd bargain and had seized it.

Yes, there was certainly humour in that.

Although Fergus's home was only a few miles from her own, Vicky had never visited it, and now, tired though she was, she looked about her with some curiosity.

It was, she knew, one of the oldest houses in that part of Cheshire, and though it was not very large nor of a very good period, she was to find that it was extremely comfortable and convenient to run. Even a casual glance made it clear that quite a lot of money had been spent on modernising it, and the decorating and furnishing had been carried out by someone who evidently knew his job. There were quite a lot of good old pieces, as Vicky was to discover later, but they and the modern stuff lived in perfect harmony because this was a home, not a museum. Yes, Vicky thought with an unconscious sigh of relief, it was certainly a place designed for people to enjoy living in. Which meant, of course, that Fergus could not have had the controlling choice. If he had, it would surely have been done in Victorian horse-hair and heavy mahogany — uncomfortably and uncompromisingly hard.

The door had been opened to them by a tall, spare woman whose first words revealed unmistakably that she came from north of the Border.

"Come away, Master Fergus, you're late!"

There was a very definite note of reproof in her tone such as one might use to a small boy come in late for a meal, and Vicky waited apprehensively for the heavens to open and Jove to thunder. But nothing of the sort happened.

Instead, Fergus gave the woman a friendly hug and said:

"Yes, I know we are, Maggie. I'm sorry. Is Mother all right?"

"She's fine," Maggie said laconically. "In her bed, but waiting for you. Away and see her, Master Fergus. I'll look after Miss Vicky!"

"Oh — yes —" Fergus turned to Vicky as if he had forgotten her presence. "Vicky, this is Maggie, who used to be my nannie and spank me with the back of a hairbrush —"

"I did no such thing, Master Fergus!" Maggie

31

interrupted indignantly. "I always used the flat of my hand — and much good it did you —"

"And now she is the mainstay of the house — and our very good friend," Fergus finished calmly, just as if she had not spoken. "Maggie, I'd like something hot after I've seen Mother — and I expect Vicky would as well —"

He left them, and walked quickly, not to the stairs as Vicky had expected, but down a corridor that turned off from the main hall.

"The mistress's rooms are downstairs," Maggie explained, evidently reading her thoughts. "Master Fergus had it arranged that way, so that on her good days she can get about on the one flat. There's nothing he wouldn't do for her. Now then," through steel-rimmed glasses a pair of shrewd eyes regarded Vicky inquiringly, "when Master Fergus comes home late like this he likes fine to come out into my kitchen. But, maybe, a young lady like yourself would prefer —"

"I'd love to come into the kitchen," Vicky said quickly. "If you don't mind —"

"I wouldn't have asked you if I minded," Maggie assured her bluntly, and led the way through a baize door to a room that, in view of the up-to-dateness of the rest of the house, was certainly a surprise. For it was a real old-fashioned kitchen, complete with an open range, a basket chair at present occupied by a sleepy tabby cat, and a table with a fringed plush table-cover. There was even a pot plant in the middle of the table, and on the wall a big printed sheet showing all the descendants of Queen Victoria, complete with photographs. Vicky drew a deep breath. At that moment, no room on earth could have looked so comforting and welcoming to her eyes, and she said with genuine enthusiasm:

"It's lovely!"

"Master Fergus let me furnish it the way I chose," Maggie explained, obviously gratified. "Here's what I call the working kitchen!"

She opened a door and Vicky had a glimpse of chromium plating and spotless tiles.

"That's nice, too," Vicky said, and Maggie nodded.

"I'm not saying it isn't — but give me a bit of old-fashioned comfort when my work's finished. Will you not take your coat off?"

Vicky slipped off the beautiful squirrel coat that had been her father's gift to her on the eve of her holiday, and laid it across one of the old wheelback chairs. The close-fitting travelling hat followed it, and then, slowly, she went over to the fire.

"Why, you're just a bairn!" Maggie said gently.

"I'm — I'm nineteen — nearly twenty," Vicky said quickly, squaring up shoulders that had drooped a little.

"That's what I said," Maggie scooped up the cat, gently pushed the girl into the chair and dropped the cat back on to her lap. "Just a bairn. Sit there and give the cat a bit cuddle while I get the soup."

She ought to offer to help, Vicky knew. She was not a guest in this pleasant house but just an employee. Somebody who was not supposed to get tired or to have personal feelings. But just for the moment it was absolutely impossible to make the effort. She had been keyed up to accept anything, no matter how unwelcoming or uncomfortable, and Maggie's kindness and the comfort of the old kitchen had been just one too many for her. Reaction, a doctor would have called it, but all Vicky knew was that she was very glad that Maggie had gone out to the farther kitchen and that a few tears did not show on a cat's fur. She stretched out her feet to the blaze and closed her eyes. And at that moment, Fergus came into the room.

Instantly she began to struggle to her feet, but Fergus motioned her still.

"Stay where you are," he said cheerfully. "Whiskers doesn't like to be disturbed once he's settled. And, incidentally, you are honoured. He doesn't condescend to any lap, let me tell you. It's a good beginning, Vicky!"

There was a friendly note in his voice that she had never heard before, and instantly she was suspicious and on the alert. It did not occur to her that, like many other men, Fergus was a totally different person in his home from what he was anywhere else. To her it was just something unfamiliar and consequently suspect.

She sat stiffly erect and silent until Maggie came in with two bowls of soup and handed one to each of them.

"That'll put new life in you," she remarked cheerfully. "Drink up every drop, now!"

Vicky murmured her thanks and Fergus said "Thanks, Maggie!" in a curt tone that was completely unlike the way he had previously spoken. Maggie looked at him thoughtfully. She had not been unaware of the strained atmosphere in the room as she had come in, and now she noticed undercurrents that she had not previously suspected.

"Master Fergus in one of his moods," was the way that she put it.

To Vicky it seemed that he was just being his ordinary self.

She did not waken the next morning until the door of her room opened and Maggie came in with a cup of tea.

"Oh!" She sat up quickly and shook her head to rid herself of the sleep that still claimed her. "Is it late, Maggie? I'm so sorry —"

"It's all right," Maggie assured her. "The mistress and I thought you'd be better for a lie-in this morning. It's barely nine o'clock."

"Nine o'clock! But that's awful!" Vicky gasped. "Mr. Imray will think I'm lazy —"

"Never fear, he's been gone an hour since!" Maggie said cheerfully, handing Vicky the cup and settling a soft shawl that she had brought on her arm round the girl's shoulders. "I'll start your bath running —"

"Maggie," Vicky said earnestly. "Please — I do appreciate your looking after me, but, you know, I'm

34

not a guest. I've got to earn my living, and I don't think Mr. Imray would like — Besides, why should you wait on me?"

The eyes of the older woman were very kindly as they rested on the small anxious face. She could have said that any woman of her age worth her salt would want to mother a child who had been hurt, but she was wise enough not to say so.

"It just comes naturally," she explained casually. "And if, whiles, you'd do as much for me, we'll get on very comfortably."

"Of course I will," Vicky promised, and sipped her tea with an easier conscience.

It was not until after breakfast that Maggie took her to see Mrs. Imray.

Vicky's heart was beating rather quickly. Supposing, in spite of Fergus's assurance that his mother approved of everything he did, Mrs. Imray did not like her? Not for a moment did she imagine that Fergus would allow her to stay here if that was the case, and then this sense of having been granted at least a breathing space, of which she had been conscious ever since she had come into the house, would vanish in a second.

But immediately she set eyes on Alice Imray her fears for herself disappeared before the claims of a far stronger emotion. Little and frail and very brave had been the way in which Fergus had described his mother, and with a sudden surge of pity Vicky realised how right he had been.

Vicky herself was not big, but she felt that she could have lifted this little wisp of a woman up in her arms. Her eyes, still intensely blue, were deep set as are the eyes of those whose sleep is disturbed by pain. There were other signs of pain, too, besides the twisted hands that lay almost uselessly on her lap. Dark rings round the blue eyes, a pointed, resolute chin that defied the worst life could do, and a strong, sweet mouth —

As soon as Vicky came into the room, Mrs. Imray's face lit in a welcoming smile.

"Come and sit where I can see you, Vicky," she said as if they were old friends. "You don't know how charming it is to have someone young and pretty to look at! Maggie and I are old women now and Fergus, dear boy, isn't like a girl! I always wanted a girl — as well as Fergus, of course. Not instead of. But perhaps it is just as well that I didn't have one, because I should have wanted to dress her up like a doll. Have you got a lot of pretty clothes?" The small head, crowned with its soft white curls, was tipped on one side like that of a small, inquisitive bird, and Vicky found herself smiling and completely at her ease.

"Yes, I have," she admitted, refusing to remember who had bought them for her and the happy times when she had worn them. "But I haven't got them with me. They were too heavy to bring in the 'plane."

"Tell me about flying," Mrs. Imray said eagerly. "Fergus says it is just like riding in a charabanc only without the scenery and with a vacuum cleaner running all the time, but I am sure there is more to it than that."

"There is the first time, anyhow," Vicky agreed. "The first time I flew it was a dull day, seen from the ground, so we went above the clouds and the sun was shining there. There were big fluffy cotton-wool clouds floating about like — like big white fish. And when the sun began to set, those in the distance turned pink and gold — it was heaven!"

"It must have been!" Mrs. Imray agreed with a deep sigh of satisfaction.

By easy stages, she brought the conversation round to the subject of Vicky's duties, and Vicky listened attentively.

"It seems very dreadful that a useless old woman who has really lived her life should be such a burden to active people like yourself and Maggie, but —" she shook her head, and momentarily her upper lip was caught between her teeth.

Something warm and loving stirred in Vicky's frozen

heart, and she took one of the small twisted hands in her own soft ones.

"Mrs. Imray, I don't think, however much people have to do for you, that you will ever be a burden. I — I shall love helping to look after you, and I hope you will like my doing it."

"You dear child!" Mrs. Imray said, considerably touched. "Of course I shall like it! I must admit, when Fergus proposed this arrangement, I was a little bit doubtful, but — he was right, as he usually is!"

She said as much to Maggie an hour later when Vicky had gone down to the village with some letters that she had written at Mrs. Imray's dictation.

Maggie nodded.

"Mp'hm," she agreed. "I had doubts myself. But she's a nice lassie! It'll work fine — though we'll have to see to it that she gets about with young people, else she'll dwine away."

"Yes," Mrs. Imray agreed thoughtfully. "We must remember that, Maggie." She was silent for a moment, but Maggie stood waiting as if she realised that everything had not been said. "It was a risk — but, as you say, Maggie, it will work. And — it is very nice that we agree about that. But — I am wondering if — everybody else will."

The eyes of the two women met in perfect understanding.

"Miss Sybil," Maggie supplied unhesitatingly, and Mrs. Imray nodded.

"Yes, Maggie, Miss Sybil!"

CHAPTER THREE

FERGUS had a busy and rather trying morning at his office. For one thing there was the accumulation of work due to his absence and for another, as Mark Pallant's solicitor and executor, there were still several officials whom he had to interview and masses of papers to go through with them. As a result of this it became evident that it would be necessary for Vicky to pay a visit to her old home in order to claim what was her own property, so that it did not get included among her father's assets.

Fergus frowned, seeing clearly that it would not be a pleasant trip for either of them; although there was one thing about it, Mark Pallant had at least shown sufficient consideration for his daughter not to end his life in his own home.

He was in the thick of it when a telephone call came through, and impatiently he lifted the receiver.

"Fergus Imray," he said shortly.

There was a soft cry of pleasure from the other end of the line.

"Oh, Fergus, you did manage it! I'm so glad! Was it all very trying?"

His frown cleared immediately.

"Sybil, my dear, I'm so glad you rang through! I fully intended ringing you as soon as I got in this morning, but there was someone waiting to see me and I haven't had a free moment since! Forgive me!"

"Of course!" said the soft rich voice. "I felt rather guilty about ringing you, but I was really rather anxious. I had to know that you were back — flying this time of the year —"

"Not very pleasant," he agreed. "However, both trips were absolutely without incident of any kind."

"And Vicky?" she asked somewhat perfunctorily. "How did she take it?"

"Pretty well, considering," he replied. "Of course, it was a shock to her —"

"It must have been," Sybil Allandyne agreed. "But really, Fergus, I don't see what else you could possibly have done to soften the blow! I mean, supposing you had been content with just sending a cablegram! And nobody could expect you to do more than that. It wasn't as if Mark was really your friend."

"No," he agreed. "Not my friend. But the sort of man for whom people always have done things — perhaps that was half the trouble. Anyhow, I felt I had to go over —"

"And I suppose Vicky took it for granted, just as her father would have done," Sybil said with a sigh. "People like that rarely appreciate the efforts other people make on their behalf. It's to be hoped she doesn't take it for granted that it is your place to continue making things easy for her. She will have to get a job —"

"I know. I told her that," he said shortly, and then, with a reluctance that he could not understand: "As a matter of fact, I've arranged one for her —"

"Oh, good!" Sybil said with genuine approval. "But I am surprised to hear you say that! I shouldn't have thought it very easy to find suitable work for a pretty little butterfly like Vicky! I hope she won't let you down!"

"No, she won't do that," Fergus was quite unaware how clearly the grim note in his voice carried over the telephone. "I shall see to that!"

"Fergus!" There was something almost like alarm in Sybil's voice. "You said that in a very odd way! Just what job is it?"

Fergus hesitated. He had looked forward to talking over the whole situation with Sybil, to having her help in solving or even preventing difficulties that were almost bound to occur where there was someone like Vicky to cope with. He had been quite sure he would have Sybil's sympathetic co-operation, and had seen no reason why he should not ask for it.

Now, suddenly, he knew that he wished to defer telling her what he had done as long as possible.

"Forgive me, Sybil, but I really mustn't stop any

longer — I've another visitor coming in five seconds — I'll tell you all about it as soon as I see you."

"Well — how about dinner tonight?" she suggested.

It was what he had fully intended proposing himself, yet now, with a hint of impatience, he found himself wishing that Sybil did not always take it for granted that he was going to discuss all his problems with her. Then he reproached himself for his ingratitude, thinking of the number of times when he had taken her interest for granted and probably bored her excessively, although she had never let him see it.

"Fine!" he said with a warmth due more to his feeling of self-criticism than because he was really anticipating the meeting with pleasure. "Same time and place?"

"Same time and place," she agreed mechanically, and hung up.

Slowly she put down the receiver and walked over to the electric fire that looked — almost — like a real one. At twenty-seven Sybil Allandyne had acquired the useful ability of looking facts unflinchingly in the face. It was a characteristic which had served her well in building up the small but expensively exclusive gown shop in Lenster during the past five years, and one which, rather uneasily, she had felt to be increasingly necessary in her dealings with Fergus.

She had come in contact with him some three years ago when she had consulted him professionally in connection with a defaulting client whose elusiveness had reached a degree where more drastic action than accounts rendered must be taken. More than likely a friendship would have resulted in any case, but it certainly helped that they discovered they were undeniably if only distantly related through their mothers.

Even before the discovery, they had fallen into the pleasant habit of dining together and going to the occasional theatre or concert, but Sybil, as clearsighted where personal matters were concerned as with her business, knew quite well that it was the tie of blood rather than anything more personal which had led to her visiting his home.

And that was the situation as it had been for nearly two years — a situation with which she had been perfectly content at first, believing that it was one capable of developing as she frankly admitted to herself that she hoped it would. She had a very genuine admiration for Fergus's ability, as she knew that he had for hers. And that mutual respect was something more necessary to Sybil in the contemplation of a possible marriage than romance. Romance, her common sense told her, might fade after having blinded you to a person's faults, but a real appreciation of basic characteristics was something reliable.

Yet now, suddenly, she felt impatient with Fergus. And the cause of her impatience was his concluding sentence. "Same time and place!"

Fergus had begun to take her for granted. Just as, to begin with, that tie of blood had made it natural for him to take her to his home, so now it made it possible for him to continue doing so without stopping to consider the interpretation which most people would have accorded the situation had it been an ordinary friendship. And yet, today, he had resented her assumption of the same privileges.

Not for a moment did she associate his mood with the fact that it had been Vicky about whom they had been talking. It was just that, man-like, he wanted privileges which he was not willing to accord her.

It was a situation which was as dangerous as it was infuriating. Either she must contrive that Fergus began to see her in a new light, or the situation would deteriorate still further. There was no half-way course. As it was, their relationship had stood still far too long. And it could not do so much longer. Every instinct told her that.

She turned and faced a full-length mirror that hung on the opposite wall, regarding herself with critical eyes. She saw a tall, slim woman with smooth golden hair. Sybil was that unusual type, a really natural blonde who did not look insipid. Her clear skin, far from being pink and white, had the ripe glow of the peach about it. Her eyes, avoiding the pale blue of so many blondes, had the changing, translucent depths of the sea in them.

And not only good to look at, but having something that mattered far more to the average man. Intense femininity and — intelligence. A rare combination, as more than one man had told her.

Other men — there had been quite a few in whom she had aroused more than a passing interest. Some four or five had proposed to her, but there had always been something that, however regretfully, made her say "No!".

She spared a passing thought for them now. Evan, who had been the best of fun but lacking common honesty. Guy, who had appreciated her looks but had no use for her brain. Tommy, who had been just exactly Guy's opposite, finding stimulation in her intelligence but not in her beauty — and so it had gone on. Not until she had met Fergus had she encountered a man who appreciated all the facets of her personality. Or who came up to her own standards.

The fact was that, in some ways, Sybil was hard to please. For one thing, she knew quite well that she could never marry a man who was not a stronger and finer personality than she herself was. Yet at the same time, he must not be so dominating that, in marrying him, she lost her personality. He must have plenty of money — but he must not mind her carrying on with her work as long as it pleased her to do so or, on the other hand, take it for granted that she was going to continue earning money indefinitely.

Well, Fergus's integrity was unassailable. Judging by the compliments he paid her, he fully appreciated her appearance. The confidences that he gave her showed his respect for her brain. Not only had he a very good practice, but from his mother he would ultimately inherit quite a lot of money. And finally, he had very definite ideas about women having ample scope to exercise their talents.

Whether Fergus had considered her qualifications as a wife in quite such detail she had no means of knowing, but whether he had or not, the way in which he sought her company had convinced her that it was only a matter of time before he asked her to marry him.

Yet now and for some weeks past, she had been conscious of a sense of insecurity.

"Oh, nonsense!" she said aloud with sudden impatience. Fergus was not the sort of man with whom one had to play the old, old game of elusiveness. He was a modern with all the clear-sightedness of his generation.

There was, of course, one very obvious reason why he might be deferring all thought of marriage for the time being. His very deep affection for his mother and the condition of her health. And yet, Sybil did not find that explanation satisfactory. If Mrs. Imray had been suffering from some complaint bound to prove fatal in a comparatively short time, that might be the explanation. But rheumatoid arthritis, however painful, was not fatal. Nor was Mrs. Imray, for all the strong tie between the two of them, in the least a possessive mother.

Sybil turned away from the glass with a shrug of the shoulders. It was useless to go around in circles as she was doing at present. She must come to some definite conclusion this evening — and somehow or other, she had a premonition that her task would not be a difficult one. That little hesitation of Fergus's when she had asked him about the job he had found for Vicky had told her that his nerves were keyed up —

It was second nature to Sybil to dress not only well but carefully. One of the greatest heart-breaks she ever had in her work was to sell a really lovely and cleverly made garment and subsequently see it worn as if it were an old sack. But never had she dressed with greater care than she did now.

For several minutes she hesitated before the big

fitted wardrobe that held, as she proudly knew, an outfit suitable for every occasion.

She was lucky. With her colouring she could wear almost any colour and know that her figure and her height would make the best of it. She considered. Fergus, coming straight from his office, would not be changing, but she felt a reluctance to go out in the trim black and white suit that she had worn all day. Suddenly she made up her mind. She wanted Fergus to realise that she had made a special effort for his benefit. She would wear something that he had not seen before — something that she had been saving up for a special occasion — and this was going to be it.

When she had first seen the material from which she had designed it, she had realised just how useful it would be. The dull black of the material had a gold thread at intervals through it. She had created a charming little ensemble which could be worn in the late afternoon, for a cocktail party or for an informal dinner. With it went a small black hat that was little more than a cap, but to one side was a sweeping bird-of-paradise plume.

When she was ready to go she faced herself again in the mirror and a slow, satisfied smile curved her rather thin lips. Fergus simply could not fail to be very much aware of her tonight! She slipped a waist-length brown squirrel cape over her shoulders and went downstairs to hail a taxi.

Her flat was over her shop and in the busiest shopping thoroughfare in Lenster, and it was only a matter of seconds before an empty taxi came along. She gave her directions with her usual clear precision, and got in.

It was not much more than a ten-minute drive to the restaurant which she and Fergus used, but in that time, shut away in the cab from the reassurance of human contacts, she suddenly realised that she was shivering, not with cold but from over-strung nerves.

Fergus stood up as she came in, and as she smiled at him, that vague sense of irritation that had been with him ever since she had telephoned vanished completely.

"My dear, you look lovely!" he said with real appreciation. "We must make this a very special occasion!"

He slipped his arm through hers and led her towards the restaurant. Fergus had a rooted objection to drinking at a bar when he had a woman companion, and Sybil, though she had no very strong feelings one way or the other, admitted that there was something to be said for the greater intimacy of talking across one's own table rather than in the busy bar where one had to raise one's voice to be heard.

She smiled now at their usual waiter as he pulled out her chair and seated her. It was delightful to be known and greeted as a valued client, and yet at the back of her mind was the thought that perhaps it might be a good idea to break new ground, to get out of a rut, however pleasant. But she would not say anything about that just yet.

"Something very special tonight, Henry," Fergus said pleasantly. "I leave it to you!"

"I will give you a meal you will never forget," Henry declared, his eyes sliding down to Sybil's left hand. No, not an engagement celebration. Still, what did that matter? Monsieur was evidently in a mood to spend! He trotted off to consult with the wine waiter, and Sybil and Fergus were left to themselves.

Fergus was smiling. Sybil had slipped off the fur cape, and he had a full view of her gown.

"Delightful!" he acknowledged warmly. "One of your own designs, of course?"

She nodded silently, conscious that Fergus's eyes were missing absolutely no detail.

"How you do it is a mystery to me, and I am content that it should be," he said at length. "For me, the finished result is sufficient! Sybil, there is no doubt about it, you are an inspired designer — and at this moment, as usual, the best possible advertisement for your own work!"

She smiled. Yet in the back of her mind was the knowledge that he had not said what she had hoped to hear. There was sincere appreciation both in what he had said and his expression as he had said it, but — there was something impersonal about it all. In spite of the trouble that she had taken over her appearance, she found herself wishing that he had paid less attention to her dress and more to herself.

Sybil was fully determined to hear the whole story of his visit to Switzerland and the outcome of it, but wisely she waited until they were half-way through their meal before she said casually:

"You sounded rather bothered when I rang up today. Did I choose an awkward time?"

She watched him intently from under half-closed lids, and saw a flicker of some emotion that she could not read pass over his lean face.

"Not particularly. The whole morning was rather bothersome."

Her eyes dropped. It had not been quite the answer she had hoped for.

"It is always difficult to leave one's work for a few days," she murmured. "Everything seems to happen the moment one's back is turned!"

He laughed shortly.

"That's true!" he agreed. "But Mark Pallant's affairs were what was bothering me most. They're in a terrible tangle, Sybil!"

"I suppose so," she agreed thoughtfully. "Is there anything left?"

"Not two ha'pennies to rub together," he declared. "In fact, there is not nearly enough left to settle all his debts. If we can manage five shillings in the pound his creditors will be lucky."

"Poor little Vicky!" Sybil said softly.

He did not answer immediately. He was toying restlessly with the handle of a knife as it lay on the table, and he did not look up as he said slowly:

"I've never, in all my life, had to do a job I

46

relished less! She has never been anything but a spoilt, irresponsible play-girl but — her father was her world, and the bottom dropped out of it when she heard what he had done."

For a brief second, Sybil dropped her hand over his.

"Poor Fergus, I think, too," she said gently.

He gave her hand a quick squeeze of gratitude.

"I had been wondering, before I telephoned to you," she went on, "whether I could do anything for her. I mean, I hear that she is a pretty child and she knows how to wear clothes — but you say you have found her a job?"

"Yes."

Suddenly alarmed, she realised that there was a note of something very much like defiance in his tone. She waited —

"I have taken her home. She is going to be a sort of companion-secretary to Mother," he explained shortly.

Involuntarily, Sybil gave a little cry.

"Fergus!"

"Yes, I expect it does surprise you," he admitted. "I must admit that I had no such idea in my mind when I last saw you, but when I saw her, it suddenly occurred to me that it solved her problem and also one of mine. Maggie is a good soul, but not only is she getting older and less able but she is not capable of doing some of the things Mother needs help for. Letter-writing, for instance. Besides, Vicky, once she gets over this shock, will cheer Mother up, I'm sure. She's a light-hearted child, and she has had plenty of experiences that will amuse Mother."

Sybil said nothing. For once in her competent life she simply did not know what to say. Fergus interpreted her silence in the most obvious way.

"You don't approve?"

"Oh — Fergus —" She spread out her hands deprecatingly. "I wouldn't go as far as that but — I do see possible dangers and difficulties —"

"Such as —?" he encouraged.

"Well — supposing Vicky turns out to be rather

47

troublesome. After all, it isn't the sort of life to which she is used. She may not do it very well — or conscientiously. And yet your mother is so sweet and compassionate. She won't want to tell you, because she will realise just how hard life is going to be for Vicky without someone to stand behind her."

Fergus shook his head.

"Don't worry about that!" he said confidently. "Believe me, I shall keep a very close watch on Miss Vicky! What else?"

She hesitated.

"There is Vicky's point of view as well. Fergus, she is very young and she has been used to having a great deal of fun in her life. Wouldn't it be wiser to find her a job where she will be with girls of her own age who have the same outlook? Your mother is a darling, Fergus. You know how fond I am of her. But she is a generation and a half older than Vicky and a sick woman besides. Is it fair to Vicky?"

This time he did not answer immediately, but at last he said slowly:

"If Vicky's life, up to the present, had been more ordinary than it has, I should agree with you. But what you have to remember is that although she has seen quite a lot of life in one sense, she has had, until now, the protection of her father's name — and his money. Now, she is a nobody, and there are quite a lot of people who will treat her accordingly."

"Even so, what does it matter to you?" she wanted to ask him, but instead she said earnestly:

"I do see that she needs someone behind her, Fergus. But — surely she has some real friends? The Ingletons, for example. She and the girl have been lifelong friends —"

"Possibly," Fergus said shortly. "But of all people, they have no use for the failures of this world, I'm sure of that!"

"I see." Well, that might be true, but why, why, *why* did it have to be Fergus who stepped into the breach?

"No, I don't think you do see." There was a grim-

48

ness in his tone that Vicky would have recognised. "Sorry though I was for the child, I was also very much annoyed with her. She was, in fact, confoundedly rude to me. Natural enough, perhaps, seeing that she has never had to accept discipline from life, never known what it means to go without anything she wants. But I am determined that she shall learn a few fundamental laws of life that will not only make it very much easier for her in the long run but which will also make her a far more pleasant person for others to have dealings with! She is going to learn to be responsible and kind to those in need, and to go without things she wants. She will not enjoy the process —"

"Nor will you, my friend!" Sybil thought with sudden amusement. It was very evident now that young Vicky had somehow contrived to get completely under his skin and that there was no love lost between them. Well, she would back Vicky — the girl simply wouldn't stand for it, as Fergus would find. Sybil was content to leave things just as they were. Before very long, Fergus would be coming to her for sympathy and rescue —

"I think that is pretty decent of you, Fergus," she said seriously. "It isn't everybody would take so much trouble. And, of course, you know that you can rely on me to do everything possible to help — the offer of a job is open if this doesn't work, for instance —"

"It's going to work!" he said stubbornly, and quite deliberately changed the subject.

It was a week before Fergus sought Vicky out and told her that he would like to have a talk with her about her father's affairs. He saw that she shrank a little, but she said "Yes, Mr. Imray," very steadily, and he knew that she would turn up at the time he suggested.

When she came into his study, he motioned her to a chair and said pleasantly:

"Just a minute, Vicky, while I finish this letter."

Vicky did as she was told. It was a comfortable leather-covered armchair that he had indicated, and in the old days, she would have lounged at her ease in it. Now she sat primly on the edge of it, her feet tidily crossed, her hands linked in her lap, the picture of demure correctness. But her eyes wandered all over the room.

During the week that she had been at Hawthornden she had been escorted by Maggie all over the house, but into this room even Maggie had only ventured to allow her a peep.

"My, if you were to hear the fuss when I tell Master Fergus that I want to spring clean his study!" she said feelingly. "But there, men are all the same! Never can find a thing if the place is decently tidy. Not that they can if it isn't. But they seem to like it that way, poor souls!"

"I'm afraid you haven't a very good opinion of men, Maggie," Vicky said gravely, and the older woman had looked at her sharply, remembering the girl's own story.

"They're all right in their way," she said hastily. "But you do no good expecting them to see things the way we women do! They're different!"

But now that she was in Fergus's room she was not thinking so much of Maggie's philosophy as taking the opportunity of inspecting the room. She sat very still, but her grey eyes took in every detail. There was a heavy mahogany desk at which Fergus was working. The chair on which he sat and several others matching it were either Chippendale or a very good copy of it. The chair in which she sat and its twin on the other side of the fireplace were modern, judging by the springing, but they must have been designed especially to go with the other furniture, so much in keeping was their appearance. There were bookshelves all along one wall, and their contents were as diverse as it was possible for books to be. From where she sat she could read the titles of several legal works, while on the shelf below were a series of detective novels. It was a very personal room, and obviously one in the arrangement of which its owner had played a large part. That made the only picture in the room all the more interesting. It was not very large. Possibly about eighteen inches by twelve. It was a pencil sketch of what looked like a stretch of wind-swept moorland. But what intrigued Vicky was not only the sense of space that it gave one, but the fact that one could *see* the wind. The rough, course grass bent over before its onslaught, but it was the trees that told one most of the story. Even if the wind were to stop blowing they would still not be erect. From the time that they had been young saplings, the wind had been blowing from the same quarter and, resigning themselves to it, they had anchored themselves with deep roots that must have demanded much of their growing power, for the trees themselves were short and stunted.

"Do you like my picture?" Fergus asked quietly, and Vicky jumped. She had completely forgotten that he was there, and now he had stolen a march on her, catching her off her guard.

"Very much," she said briefly.

He went over to it and stood gazing at it.

"It's the view from one of the windows of the house I have in Anglesey," he told her. "We live there in the summer. At least, my mother and Maggie do. I go down at week-ends."

"I see," Vicky said politely.

"I think you will like it, Vicky," he said, still without turning. "One gets the same feeling of space and cleanness that there is in Switzerland. Of course, in the winter it is uncomfortably bleak — the wind stings your eyes and you can lean against it as if it were a solid support."

She did not reply, and after a moment he came back to his desk, swinging his chair round so that he faced her.

He had said that he wanted to talk to her about her father's affairs, but he did not seem to be in any hurry to begin. Instead, looking at her curiously, he asked:

51

"Well, Vicky, how has this first week gone?"

Vicky sat tongue-tied. The truth was that this house of his to which he had brought her had been a sanctuary to her. Not, she hurriedly told herself, because of anything that he had done, for she had hardly set eyes on him, but because she had been busier than she had ever been in her life in conditions different from any which she had ever known. To her own amazement, she had found not only her time but her mind fully occupied by her new life, so that there had been times when she had been quite happy — until she remembered.

"It has gone — quite well," she admitted.

"Good!" he said heartily. "You have certainly cheered up my mother quite a lot!"

"Have I?" she said more eagerly than she realised. "I'm glad!" She hesitated momentarily. "Mr. Imray — will she never be any better?"

He shook his head.

"No, Vicky," he said shortly.

Vicky turned her face away from him.

"It must be dreadful for you to see her like that," she said almost under her breath. "But — it could be worse for you. She is very — brave."

He could have told her that it was just that bravery which wrung his heart, but he held the words back, knowing that she was thinking of someone who had not been brave.

There was a silence in the room, and it was not until a falling coal broke it that Fergus stirred and said briskly:

"Now, Vicky, we must get down to business —"

But Vicky interrupted him.

"Please, I want to ask you something first. It's about the money that Mother left me, has — has that gone?"

He hesitated.

"I'm afraid so. In fact, all that is left is — your personal belongings at Mount View and the jewellery which your mother left you."

Vicky flinched. Ever since Mrs. Ingleton had

brought the subject up she had been hoping against hope that her mother's money at least was left, not so much for the sake of the partial independence that it would give her as because, if it had gone, it was another horrible thing to have to know. It had been money for her which her mother had left in care of her father. And now she knew the worst. It had gone, too.

"I want you to come over to Mount View with me one day soon," Fergus said in a businesslike way. "We shall meet one of the Receiver's officials and you must formally claim any property that is yours —"

"No!" Vicky said sharply. "That is what I wanted to say to you. Except for my clothes — I don't want anything. Whatever there is can be sold! And the jewellery. I should like you to sell it and repay yourself for the trip to Switzerland and my hotel bill. The rest can go to — the creditors. I — I couldn't bear to have it!"

CHAPTER FOUR

VICKY, too emotionally disturbed by her declaration
to keep still, had stood up as she spoke, and now
Fergus did the same. Gazing into that young, pain-
twisted face, the pity that he had always felt for her
since tragedy had touched her was paramount in his
mind.

"Poor child!" He laid his hand gently on her
shoulder, but instantly Vicky shrank away from his
touch.

"I don't want your pity!" she said stonily. "It
is just a matter of business! My father owed money.
It isn't right that I should keep things which his
money bought."

He was silent for a moment; then he motioned her
back to her chair.

"Sit down, Vicky," he said in a preoccupied voice.

She obeyed him because suddenly it seemed as if
her legs were about to buckle under her. He did not
go on talking immediately, but she saw that he was
pondering over what she had said, and for the moment she was glad to have an opportunity of regaining
her self-control.

"Now look, Vicky," he said at length, "I appreciate your feelings in this matter, but I have got to
make the situation quite clear to you. That is only
right. First of all, if your father made you any really
expensive presents very recently, then his creditors
may have some claim on them. That, you see, is
logical enough. A man, knowing that such a situation
was rapidly coming to a head, might otherwise put
everything that he had in the name of his wife or
daughter and so defraud his creditors. Do you understand?"

Vicky nodded.

"Father gave me my fur coat just before I left
for Switzerland. And this for my last birthday." She
stripped off the little diamond watch and laid it down

on his desk. "Last Christmas he paid for me to go over to America to visit some friends there — and before that —"

Fergus interrupted her.

"That's far enough back, I think, Vicky," he said quietly. "Well, that's one side of the situation. The other is that any property which is yours having been given to you by anyone else remains yours absolutely. The jewellery you speak of. Was that your mother's?"

"Yes. But Father gave her most of it," Vicky said, her voice now perfectly under control. "So you see, it comes to the same thing."

"Not quite. You see, Vicky, you are still under age. Whether you have the right to dispose of valuable property like that while you are still a minor is something that must be gone into. I cannot give you an opinion out of hand. And that brings up another matter. As you know, I was your father's solicitor. I am also his executor. None the less, if you prefer it, your affairs can be put in the hands of some other solicitor, although I am perfectly willing to see to your business for you."

"Have I got any business?" Vicky asked with sudden bitterness. "And how should I pay you?"

"Out of what you earn," he suggested calmly. "And, by the way, that reminds me. You have been here a week now —"

He took out his wallet and counted out some notes. "Here are your wages!"

Reluctantly Vicky held out her hand and Fergus put the crisp notes into it.

"Thank you," she muttered.

"Count them," he suggested. "You must learn to be businesslike, Vicky!"

With a slight shrug, she did as he told her.

"You've made a mistake, Mr. Imray," she said in a cold, precise little voice. "You've given me more than we agreed on." She held out some notes to him.

"I told you that I was perfectly willing to pay more for the right person," he said, making no effort to take it from her. "And, as I have said, I am very well pleased with the way in which you have cheered my mother up. Take your money, Vicky, you have earned it!"

But she still held out her hand towards him.

"Just now I told you that I did not want pity, Mr. Imray," she said obstinately. "I don't want charity either! Please take the money."

And then, as he still made no attempt to take it, she allowed it to flutter down on to his desk.

"Is there anything else, Mr. Imray?" she asked quietly.

"Yes. Although you feel so strongly about the disposal of your possessions, I shall have to ask you to come with me to Mount View some day soon —" He took out his pocket diary. "Next Tuesday afternoon would suit me —"

"Very well," she agreed.

"That's all, then, Vicky."

But she did not immediately turn away, and Fergus, who had turned back to his letter, looked up at her.

"Yes, Vicky?"

"I want you to tell me just what happened," she said hardly.

Slowly he shook his head.

"Vicky, you're tormenting yourself —" he began, but she cut across his words.

"I've got to know," she said through clenched teeth. "I suppose it was all in the papers, but afterwards, no one seemed to know what had happened to that one that Glenda had —"

Fergus, who could have told her exactly what had happened to it, dropped his eyes to the small glittering watch that lay in front of him.

"As far as we know, your father must have realised just how bad things were late one afternoon. He came home before he was expected, but went out again in the car. He drove quite a distance — the tank was quite empty, and then —"

"He shot himself?" Vicky said in a small frozen voice.

Fergus looked at her sharply.

"Who told you that?" he demanded.

"I guessed. You said that it had been quick —" Suddenly he saw that her throat was working convulsively, and without another word, she fled out of the room.

For a long time, Fergus sat very still. He had a lot to think about, for in these last few moments he had realised several things that he had not done before. He had known right from the beginning that he was taking on a difficult job in trying to help Vicky, but he had not had an inkling that it would turn out to be quite such a complex problem.

He picked up Vicky's little watch. It had looked very pretty on her slim wrist, and yet she had torn it off as if it had burnt her.

He opened a drawer and took out an envelope. Into it he put the watch and carefully sealed it. Then, with a thoughtful expression on his face, he went to the small wall safe and carefully shut it away there.

Just before she had gone into Fergus's study Vicky had put a heavy coat on a chair outside the door. Now, as she ran out of his room, she was thankful for her foresight. The one thing in the world that she wanted was to be utterly alone.

She snatched up the coat and, slinging it round her shoulders, raced down the trim gravel drive. There was a masked, unseeing look about her eyes, but even so she had a definite destination in view. From her bedroom window she had seen, across one or two fields, a small wood that, stripped of leaves though it was at this time of year, would form some sort of a barrier between herself and the people in the house she had just left so hastily.

The leaves scrunched with a pleasing crispness beneath her feet, and there was a clean autumn-perfumed wind blowing. Unconsciously Vicky's spirits began to lift, and, picking her way carefully, she began to run.

In a short time she had reached the other side of the wood and instantly there was a feeling of spaciousness. She was standing at the top of a slight rise, and from it she had a view of the Welsh hills, smudged and purple in the distance.

Vicky drew a deep breath and stood there, silently drinking it in. She was content for the moment simply to identify herself with the beauty and solitude of the place, but how long that mood might have lasted she had no time to find out for, unexpectedly, there came a summons.

"Hi! Lend a hand, will you?"

It was a man's voice and it came from the field adjacent to the one in which Vicky stood. She might have regretted the presence of another human being, but there was a note of urgency in the voice, and, without stopping to think, she made her way as quickly as possible over the rough field to a five-barred gate. It was padlocked, but she scrambled over and immediately saw what the trouble was.

Near to the gate a young man in riding breeches sat on the ground holding his ankle in his hands, and at some distance a horse was kicking up its heels in obvious enjoyment.

"Had a toss?" Vicky asked sympathetically.

The boy on the ground — he was little more — grinned ruefully.

"And how!" he agreed feelingly. "Serves me right! I knew perfectly well that Buck was fresh — he doesn't get enough exercise — and I let my attention wander —" In spite of the pain that he was suffering, the admiration in his face told her quite clearly that it was the unexpected sight of herself in the next field that had distracted him.

"I'd better pull your boot off —" Vicky began, but he shook his head.

"I was wondering if you could possibly fetch someone who could catch Buck," he suggested diffidently. "I know it's a bit of nerve to put you to the bother, but if you did, I think I could mount all right. It's my right ankle I've hurt, you see."

Vicky slipped her coat off.

"I'll catch him," she said confidently, and before the boy could protest, she was off.

Buck regarded her suspiciously, but Vicky, her hands in her jacket pockets, came unhurriedly towards him.

"Hallo!" she said cheerfully. "You're a bad lot, aren't you?"

Buck evidently liked the sound of her voice, for he cocked his head inquiringly and, to her relief, Vicky saw that it was high spirits and not vice that had prompted the rebellion.

She stood still now but kept on talking, and gradually Buck's curiosity was aroused. He came a little closer and Vicky held out her hand.

"Come on, you big silly!" she said affectionately.

Just what happened after that the boy who was watching hardly knew, but the next minute, in spite of the handicap of a skirt, Vicky was up in the saddle and Buck was trotting sedately towards his master.

But suddenly Vicky changed her mind. It was going on for two months since she had been in the saddle, and sudden exhilaration possessed her. She understood Buck's mood of revolt — and shared it.

"Come on, Buck!" she said urgently, and gave the merest touch to the sensitive creature's flanks. Buck responded instantly. First a canter, then a gallop —

Just for a second Vicky felt a twinge of conscience. She had no right to be doing this without having first asked Buck's owner for permission; but she need not have worried. The boy had contrived to pull himself into an upright position and now, holding on to the gate, he was cheering Vicky on. Twice Buck circled the field, then Vicky, completely mistress of the situation, came thundering down straight at the practice jump in the middle. Over it sailed Buck, and Vicky, exhilarated to a point of recklessness, wheeled and took the jump again. Twice more they cleared it easily, Vicky not so much needing to encourage Buck as simply give him his head. And in her ears, the cheers of her audience rang like sweet music.

"Oh, you're a darling!" she told Buck, leaning forward to fondle him. "I could ride you all day, but we had better go back to your master now — and don't you get throwing him again! Understand? I won't have it!"

Buck whinnied as if he understood, and trotted quietly over to the gate on which his master was now sitting.

"I say, you're marvellous!" he said enthusiastically. "I've never seen anyone ride like it — and Buck doesn't take to everyone, either!"

Vicky slid down from the saddle and tethered Buck to the gatepost before she answered.

"I've ridden all my life," she said slowly. "But I don't suppose I shall be doing much more."

"Hard up?" her companion asked sympathetically. "Aren't we all! Still, you never know your luck!"

"I know mine," Vicky said simply.

The boy stared at her thoughtfully.

"You know, I've never really met you before, and yet I'm quite sure I know you by sight. Do you live in the district?"

"Yes," Vicky said shortly. "My name is Vicky Pallant, if that helps."

"Mine is Gil Pickard," he said promptly. Then she saw a startled look come into his frank face. "Pallant? You — you don't mean —" his voice trailed away and Vicky, the exaltation of such a short time ago completely gone, dug her hands deep into her pockets.

"Yes. His daughter," she said stonily. "And now, if you are ready, I'll help you mount."

"Here, wait a minute —" Gil expostulated. "Golly, of all the blundering oafs — listen, Vicky, I could kick myself —"

"Why?" she asked indifferently. "It's the most natural thing in the world for you to be — rather shocked. I'm used to it — and to people thinking it is wiser not to be friends with me because I'm — broke."

"If that's all that's worrying you," Gil said cheerfully, "so am I! Here, come and sit on this gate with me. I've got a couple of apples in my pocket. Have one?"

Silently Vicky took the apple from him and scrambled up beside him on the gate. They munched in a silence that was at once companionable and understanding. Then, as if moved by a single thought, they threw their cores to Buck and turned to look at one another.

"Go on, get it off your chest," Gil advised paternally. "You'll feel much better if you do!"

Vicky's eyes dropped.

"If you can't guess, there's nothing to tell," she muttered.

Gil slipped a friendly arm round her shoulders.

"I suppose I can, really," he admitted. "As sore as hell — and aching to escape from your own thoughts. That's why riding Buck gave you such a kick!"

"Yes. Oh, *yes!*" she agreed eagerly. "How did you know?"

"Got a bit of imagination," he told her. "That's the way I'd feel about it myself. Only you can't escape by trying to run away from it, Vicky. And it doesn't do you any good, either, to keep on bashing your head up against a brick wall of facts."

"What can you do, then?" she asked, spreading out her hands in a gesture of despair.

Gil caught the one nearer to him and inspected it gravely.

"What uncommonly nice hands you've got, Vicky," he said approvingly. "So many girls have such chunky, solid hands, but yours are slim and your fingers taper — the sort of hand that ought to hold a fan — or perhaps toy negligently with a rose. A red one, for choice!"

In spite of herself Vicky laughed as she gently drew her hand from his clasp and Gil promptly grabbed it back.

"That's it, Vicky! That's what you've got to do!"

"What?" she asked, startled at his earnestness.

"Well —" he said more slowly. "I know what I mean inside me, but it may take a bit to get it out. It was you laughing, although a minute or so before you were in the dumps — yes, that's it! You're young, Vicky. Young enough to have lots of facets to your character. Well, you've got to see to it that the one you keep turned up is the one that is most fun —or — Lord, I'm making a mess of this!"

"No, go on!" Vicky commanded.

"Well —" he plunged again. "There is the past — you can't deny it, because it has happened. It's on record, so to speak. Beastly things happened in it to you. First of all, you've got to see if there is anything you can do to make them less beastly."

"I have," she said quickly. "I've got — not money but things — I'm selling them and putting the money in with anything of Father's."

"Oh, nice work!" he approved softly. It did not seem to strike either of them as strange that, on such a very short acquaintance, they were able to talk so confidentially, and he went on: "Of course, worldly people would tell you that you are very silly not to hang on to every penny that you can claim, but — you're not, you know. It's the best possible thing you could have done to help yourself out of this slough of despond — what's the matter?"

For Vicky's soft lips had shaped themselves into a round "O" of surprise.

"I've just been thinking — it's odd. Father always said that Mr. Imray was very close-fisted and yet, when I told him what I wanted to do, he thought it was a good idea, too."

"Imray? The chap that lives in the house the other side of the wood?" Gil asked. "What's he got to do with it?"

"He was Father's solicitor. Now — I work for him. I'm a sort of companion-secretary to his mother," Vicky explained shortly.

"I see," Gil said slowly. "Well, there's one thing, you're as safe as houses there. I mean — he's a thoroughly decent sort — or so my uncle says. Never met him myself."

"Never mind him now," Vicky dismissed Fergus casually. "Go on with what you were saying."

"Oh — where had I got to? About seeing if there is anything you can do to make it less beastly, wasn't it? Well, after that there is only one thing for it, Vicky. You have got to put a barrier between yourself and the past. And there is only one thing that can make such a barrier."

"What, Gil?" she asked eagerly.

"The present," he told her earnestly. "Vicky, you've got to fill the present up with things happening. And more than that, you've got to plan things for the future so that there is always something to look forward to —"

"Yes," she agreed slowly. "But how? You see, I haven't any friends now —"

"Well, you have, if I am any good," he declared. "No, wait a minute, Vicky. You've got to get this quite clear. I'm not rich and I never shall be. Like you, I've had — reverses — though not as grim as yours. It was just that father died rather young and instead of becoming a barrister, as we had planned, I've got a job in a bank. I expect you know my uncle — he's Sir Giles Tenby. A decent old stick, but he can't do anything for me. For one thing, this place of his takes every penny he can find, and for another, he's got two sons who naturally take precedence of me. Not but what I am always made welcome when I come down here, and there is quite a bit of fun going — and that's how I know you've got to take all the fun that is offered to you. I mean, wouldn't I be rather dumb to refuse a ride on Buck just because I know I'll never be able to own a horse like that myself?"

"Yes —" Vicky agreed, her forehead wrinkled in her effort to follow him. "But that isn't quite like me —"

"Not quite but — near enough. Look, you must have time off. Well, arrange it so that it is at the week-end or evenings, and we'll do things together. Go to a cinema or queue for the cheap seats at the theatre, or go for a tramp — if that's any good to you," he finished with sudden humility. "I haven't got enough money to paint the town red, you know. It won't be like you've been used to."

"I don't want it to be," Vicky said with deep conviction. "But — it isn't so easy as that! I — I don't know if I have any time off. Nobody has said anything about it!"

"Oh, I say, this day and age!" Gil protested. "What is this chap's name, anyway? Imray — or Rochester? Because the sooner he makes up his mind, the better! You're no Jane Eyre, my child, and I'm going to see he knows it! I suppose he hasn't got a mad wife shut up anywhere, has he?" he asked suspiciously.

Vicky giggled because it was so nice to be silly and frivolous — and also because the idea of Fergus Imray having a skeleton in the cupboard really was quite idiotic.

"You are a chump!" she said with something like genuine affection in her voice. "Anyway, there's one thing, I'm not likely to fall in love with *this* Mr. Rochester. Or he with me, for that matter," she added candidly.

Gil shot a sideways glance at her. He wasn't so sure on that last point, but anyway, what did it matter? They sat in easy silence for a time, and then Vicky said earnestly:

"You know, I'm glad you've had a rotten time!"

"Well, there's a nice thing!" he retorted.

"No, I don't mean it like that. I mean — something like this has to happen to you before you can possibly understand. I know that. If this had happened to one of my friends — Glenda Ingleton, for example — I just shouldn't have known what to do about it. I should have felt it was the sort of thing that happened to other people but never to oneself. But you — you really understand. And you're quite right. The only thing for me is to skim along on the surface — snatch all the happiness I can. It doesn't

really mean that one is hard or heartless. Only —"
her voice broke — "there isn't any sense in constantly taking off a bandage to see if the wound has
healed, is there?"

"Not a bit," he agreed heartily. "And then, when
it *is* time to take it off — maybe you'll find it has
healed — quite a bit."

"Anybody else would have said 'healed right up',"
Vicky commented. "Only — you know, don't you?"

"I do!" he agreed cheerfully. "And now, sweet,
if you don't mind, I'll get you to give me a leg up.
I think I'd better take this ankle of mine home as
quickly as possible, because, at present, it's doing
its best to burst its way out of my boot — I ought
to have let you pull it off first of all."

Vicky brought Buck as near as she could to the
gate and then, with a little help from her, Gil managed to mount, though his face was rather white at
the end of the effort.

"Would you like me to walk back with you?"
Vicky asked anxiously, but he would not hear of it.

"You pop along back and have it out with Imray
about your time off," he advised. "And I'll ring you
up this evening!"

"I'll see about it as soon as I get back to the
house!" Vicky promised.

But she did not have to wait as long as that.

She tramped back up the rising ground, and at
the verge of the little wood, she came face to face
with Fergus Imray.

One glance told her that he was extremely angry,
and his first words confirmed it.

"Where the devil have you been?" he demanded.
"Do you know I've spent the best part of an hour
searching for you?"

Only an hour or so ago Vicky would have sought
to placate him, fearing that if she did not, he might
send her packing before she had time to find another
job. But now, rather excitingly, she found that she
was not afraid any more.

"But why?" she asked innocently.

"Why?" He stared at her as if he thought she had taken leave of her senses. "Surely that is clear enough? You left me abruptly in — considerable distress, and apparently vanished. Maggie was very much worried, and I had no choice but to come and hunt for you."

"I'm sorry Maggie was worried," Vicky said with deceptive gentleness. "But I'm afraid that you must accept the responsibility for that — as well as for having had to waste your time!"

"*I* must accept —" he repeated, his voice chilly with displeasure. "I must ask you to explain just what you mean!"

"Very well!" Vicky agreed, hoping that she sounded calmer than she felt. "I've been in your house nearly a week now, and you yourself said that you were satisfied with me. Yet you haven't suggested that I should take a single hour off duty — nor made arrangements for me to do so in the future! That being so, you mustn't be surprised if I snatch an odd hour or so sometimes to see — my friends!"

"I understood that you had no friends — on your own statement," Fergus said stiffly. "Consequently, it did not occur to me that it would be a kindness to insist on your taking any time off until you yourself suggested it — as you have done now. I shall be obliged if you will come straight back to the house, so that there is no chance of my mother being alarmed, but as soon as we are there, we can discuss the matter."

Without another word he turned and led the way back, giving Vicky no choice but to follow. She did so without protest, but inwardly she was seething with indignation at the way in which he had contrived to evade all responsibility and lay it on her shoulders instead. And, if the truth were told, her indignation was all the more intense because, in her heart of hearts, she knew that he was perfectly right. She had to admit that she had asked nothing more than to have her time fully occupied with work that she

66

could not avoid, and that she would not have known what to do with free time if she had had it.

But if only he wouldn't be so inevitably, so infuriatingly right! To be wrong now and again would be such an endearingly human quality — not, of course, that it mattered to her whether he was human or not.

They did not speak again until they reached the house, and Fergus, after opening the door, stood aside for her to pass. Then Vicky murmured, "Thank you!" and slipped inside.

Maggie, hearing the sound, came out to greet them, and Fergus said quickly:

"It's all right, Maggie, Miss Vicky just went for a walk!"

"Just what I told you!" Maggie said calmly. "The lassie's more sense than you credit her with!"

Vicky looked quickly from one to the other of them. From the way in which Maggie spoke one might have thought that it was not she but Fergus who had been worried by her absence, but, of course, that was nonsense. Doubtless it was just Maggie's way of pretending that she had not made a fuss.

Fergus, however, made no comment and led the way, not to his study but to the little sitting-room that they used in preference to the large drawing-room when there were no visitors in the house.

"Now then, Vicky, tell me what it is you want," he said pleasantly.

If he had fought her, if he had appeared to grudge her what was, after all, her right, she would have felt more at her ease, but as it was she blurted out:

"Can I go out on Saturdays — and sometimes week-day evenings?" with all the gaucheness of a schoolgirl.

"Saturdays, yes," he said promptly. "Other evenings — not until I come home."

"But that's not until seven — later than that, sometimes," Vicky protested. "By the time I had got to Lenster it wouldn't be any good."

Fergus shook his head.

"I'm sorry, Vicky, but that cannot be helped. You can have time off during the day — no?" as Vicky shook her head. "I'm sorry."

"But why, Mr. Imray?" Vicky demanded. "I don't want to be unreasonable —"

Fergus's heavy brows lifted.

"Don't you?"

"Of course I don't!" Vicky insisted, colouring a little. "But it seems to me that *you* are being very unreasonable — you don't even tell me why —"

Fergus regarded her thoughtfully.

"No, I don't feel called on to give you my reason," he admitted.

"And yet you expect me to say 'Yes, Mr. Imray, certainly, Mr. Imray!' as meekly as if I were a child!" she rushed on.

Fergus shook his head and she saw that his stern mouth was curved in a very slight smile.

"Oh, no, Vicky! The last thing I expect is for you to be meek where taking orders is concerned," he told her calmly. "On the contrary, I expect you to fight every inch of the way. But I must warn you, I intend to fight as well! And — I am confident that in the end I shall win!"

CHAPTER FIVE

HE WAS so sure of himself! So infuriatingly certain that he knew best! Particularly where women were concerned. Evidently he regarded them as an inferior creation whose opinion was worthless. But now, if never before, he had met someone who was not going to bow to his ruling just because he happened to think that she should.

"I would not be too sure of that, Mr. Imray," Vicky said softly.

"But I am. Quite sure," he declared calmly and maddeningly.

"You can't be," she contradicted flatly. And then, curiously: "What makes you so sure?"

His brown eyes rested thoughtfully on her flushed, angry young face.

"Because, Vicky, though you are undisciplined and somewhat unpredictable, you are none the less basically sound. I believe, too, that you have some idea of fair play. Consequently, in time you will come to realise that I am justified in stipulating the times when you will be out of the house, and, when that happens, you will be fair enough to admit it."

It was the last reason that she had expected him to give, and Vicky found herself without anything to say. Admittedly it was a compliment that had something of a sting in it, but none the less, it was a compliment. She hardly knew whether she was pleased or annoyed by it.

"Well?" Fergus asked after a moment's silence.

Vicky hesitated. With a sense of grudging admiration she realised now just how clever he had been. If she were to defy him it would be tantamount to admitting that his opinion of her was incorrect — that she was neither — what was it he had said — basically sound nor capable of fair play.

"I think that you are asking a good deal, Mr. Imray," she said slowly at length. "But — I promise that I will not go against your wishes — except for some very good reason."

She was leaving herself a very big loophole and she wondered whether he would realise it and, still more, whether he would allow her to get away with it.

That he did see she had found the one way to out-manoeuvre him was perfectly evident. There was a sudden glint in his brown eyes — though whether it was caused by admiration for her astuteness or simply by amusement she had no means of knowing.

"Very well, Vicky, we will leave it at that. I rely on your good judgment! I shall be bringing a guest home with me for the week-end, but that need not make any difference. Make what arrangements you choose. You have a key, haven't you?"

"Yes," Vicky said, rather subdued at the way in which a first-class fight seemed to have fizzled out to nothing at all. "Maggie gave me one."

"Right! That's all then, isn't it? Unless you have anything else you want to discuss?"

"No —" Vicky said slowly. "Yes! Have you any objection to my making or receiving telephone calls?"

"None whatever," he responded promptly. "Provided you keep them within reasonable limits. I don't like the telephone to be engaged for half an hour or so at a time. And if you want to make long-distance calls, I should like to know — either before or afterwards."

"Very well," Vicky agreed and, feeling herself dismissed, went slowly out of the room.

It was almost time for her to go to Mrs. Imray's room to read aloud to her, and mechanically Vicky went to her own room first to change her damp shoes and wash her hands.

Finally she brushed and combed her dark silky hair, and found herself falling into a sort of reverie.

Fergus — Gil. What different types they were! And not only because there was a gap of possibly eight to ten years between them. About Gil there was something youthfully gallant that made a very quick appeal to an answering chord in her own make-up. But Fergus — she puckered her lips thoughtfully — for the first time she found herself experiencing a reluctant appreciation of his brains. Those he undeniably had. And they ruled his outlook. With Gil, she could well believe that it was his heart which governed everything he did. Which made him so — so — she hesitated. Lovable was the word which had come immediately into her mind, yet could she apply it to an acquaintance whom she had only met for the first time an hour or so ago? But it was true, none the less. Whereas the word one instinctively applied to Fergus was "reliable". Not by any stretch of the imagination could one call him lovable.

As she went slowly down to Mrs. Imray an errant thought flashed into her mind.

She could not imagine Fergus arousing any affection in her. But would she find that Gil could be completely reliable? Or were the two qualities completely irreconcilable?

She dismissed the thought immediately because it seemed disloyal to her new friend, but in her ignorance she did not know that such a thought, once having been given birth, is not so easily destroyed as that, though it may seem to be. As though it were a being separate from oneself, it can come back unbidden at any time.

In spite of Fergus's permission for her to use the telephone, Vicky was on tenterhooks that evening.

There was a good play on the television and Mrs. Imray and Fergus apparently found it absorbing, but Vicky found it very difficult to concentrate.

They sat in a deceptively family-like little group, Mrs. Imray propped up on the day couch which Fergus had wheeled in, Fergus looking rather well in the formal black and white of his dinner suit, herself in a half-afternoon, half-dinner dress that she had never really liked just because it was such an indeterminate affair — such a scene as there must be in hundreds of homes. And yet, with a difference. Be-

71

tween mother and son there was undoubtedly a strong mutual bond of affection and understanding, though Vicky gave the credit for it to Mrs. Imray rather than Fergus. But she, though she was included in the little circle, was not really of it. An outsider —

She heard the telephone bell ring and half rose, convinced that it must be Gil, but Fergus motioned her to sit down again.

"I'll take it," he said quietly. "I am expecting a call —"

Vicky sank down again. She could not tell him that she too was expecting a call, but she sat taut and strained, unconscious of Mrs. Imray's kindly, curious eyes, until Fergus returned.

"It is for you, Vicky. I have put it through to my study."

Vicky murmured her thanks and slipped out of the room.

Fergus had left the light on in the study, and Vicky ran eagerly over to the desk, though she was careful to shut the door behind her.

"Hallo?" said a voice as soon as she picked up the instrument.

"Oh, it *is* you, Gil!" she exclaimed, unaware of the relief in her voice.

"Of course it is!" he retorted. "Didn't Imray tell you who it was? He was very careful to ask me my name!"

"Was he?" Vicky said, suddenly troubled. "And yet he didn't tell me! How queer. I wonder why —"

There was a little silence.

"Curiosity, perhaps!" Gil suggested. "Still, never mind that. How did things go? Did you get anything fixed up?"

"Yes! Saturday evenings. But not weekdays. Mr. Imray was very definite about that. At least, he said he didn't want me to go out until he was home."

"Oh!" Gil appeared to digest this. "Well, it's a beginning, anyway! Let's make the best of it! This Saturday?"

"Please!" Vicky said eagerly. "Only — Dutch treat, please, Gil!"

She heard his soft chuckle.

"Bless the infant, how she is learning! Not this first time, Vicky. It's something special. But after that, if you like — at least sometimes!"

"All right," she agreed. "What shall we do?"

"Well — how about leaving that to me? Put on a pretty dress — not evening things, though. And I'll come and collect you at half-past five. All right?"

"All right," she agreed. "Except — would you mind very much if I met you at the gates? I promise I won't keep you waiting about — but —"

She hesitated, wondering if she had put things so clumsily that he would think that, for any reason, she was ashamed of their friendship, but Gil understood without any difficulty.

"I get you! Your employer is just a little bit too inquisitive about your affairs?"

"Well —" Perhaps it was not really fair to say that, but it was better for Gil to imagine that was just what she meant than that she should try to explain something she had not really got clear in her own mind.

They exchanged a few more words and then Vicky rang off and went back to the sitting-room. Somewhat to her confusion, the play was over and Fergus had turned on the lights again, with the result that there was no chance of her slipping quietly back into her seat and, in the half dark, avoiding any curious glances.

But neither Mrs. Imray nor Fergus made any comment. They were discussing the play they had just seen, and very briefly Fergus gave Vicky an account of the part that she had missed. Then it was time for him to wheel his mother back to her room. For a while after Mrs. Imray had gone to bed, Vicky sat talking to her. More than once it was on the tip of the girl's tongue to tell this sweet-faced, gentle woman of her new friendship and what it meant to her, but one thing prevented it. One could hardly speak of it without, in some way, appearing to criticise Fergus. And however much one might do that in one's heart, it was impossible to do it to his mother. Particularly as, whatever his attitude might be to other people, to his mother he showed nothing but kindness and consideration.

But that night, Vicky went to bed with a lighter heart than she had known since Fergus had told her of her father's death.

Yet, strangely enough, her sleep was troubled by dreams that left her with a feeling of having barely avoided some terrible catastrophe, although they were so vague that in the morning she could hardly remember them.

The week-end visitor of whom Fergus had spoken to Vicky turned out to be Sybil Allandyne.

It was Maggie who first mentioned the fact, and Vicky looked at her sharply. There was something in her tone which suggested, if not a dislike for Sybil, at least a lack of actual liking.

"Oh, I know her!" Vicky commented. "At least, *of* her. She has that very smart dress shop in Lenster, hasn't she? I have never bought anything from her because, of course, her things are for older women."

"She makes her own things, so I gather," Maggie announced non-committally.

"Well, she isn't very young herself, is she?" Youth asked arrogantly. "Quite thirty or thirty-five!"

"She's twenty-seven. She told me so herself," Maggie replied, but there was no reproof in her voice.

"Oh!" Vicky said indifferently. "Well, there's not much difference, is there?"

Maggie laughed.

"You'll likely think so when you get there yourself," she suggested dryly.

Vicky shrugged her shoulders. It seemed such a long way off!

"Is she a friend or a relation — or what?" she asked with casual interest.

"Some sort of a relation. A distant one. Not but what Master Fergus takes a considerable interest in Miss Sybil!"

"Oh!" Vicky asked more alertly. "Are they engaged — or going to be?"

"We—ll —" Maggie said with somewhat belated caution. "I wouldn't like to say 'yes' and I wouldn't like to say 'no'! Myself, I'd say things are just the way that they might go either way! They're certainly very good friends!"

"Oh!" Vicky screwed her face up expressively. "How dull! If I were going to marry anyone, I'd want them to be able to sweep me right off my feet so that I didn't know whether I was standing on my head or my heels!"

"And like enough, when you got yourself sorted, you'd find maybe he had a squint or was awful mean! I ken this love business fine!" Maggie's sniff was a triumph of disdain.

Vicky glanced down at the work-worn hands and the broad gold band on the left hand.

"You've been married, haven't you, Maggie?" she asked gently, and the woman nodded.

"Three times!" she announced with considerable pride. "And nobody can say I made a poor wife, for I buried each one of them real well! No stint, believe me!"

"I'm sure there wasn't," Vicky agreed, stifling a laugh with considerable difficulty. Then, changing the subject in a desperate effort not to disgrace herself, "When does Miss Allandyne come?"

"Oh, she'll come down with Master Fergus on Friday evening," Maggie predicted carelessly. "Likely they'll do some theatre or other first and come down late. And, see here, Miss Vicky —" she paused, evidently considering the wisdom of going on at all.

"Yes, go on, Maggie. I — I think you want to say something confidential and you're not quite sure if you can trust me. Isn't that it?"

"Aye, that's it!" Maggie admitted.

"Well, you are the best judge of that, Maggie, but — you *can*, you know!"

"I'll take a chance," Maggie said philosophically, if not very complimentary. "It's just this. Miss Sybil is not the sort of young lady who tolerates any interference in her plans!"

"That's — interesting," Vicky said slowly. "But I don't see how it concerns me!"

"Mind and see she knows that!" Maggie advised dryly. And went off about her work leaving Vicky considerably puzzled as to why the warning had been given to her of all people.

Maggie's confidences had served to make Vicky both cautious, and curious to see Sybil. It was not that she was in the least interested in whether the visitor was ultimately to be Fergus's wife or not from any personal point of view — why should she be? And that being so, a clever business woman like Sybil would know from her manner that she had nothing to fear from a mere companion.

None the less, Sybil, whether as a friend or fiancée, was certain to have quite a lot of influence with Fergus and interest in the way his home was run. Or she might come to the conclusion that Vicky was not good for Mrs. Imray in her frail condition. There were quite a lot of pitfalls.

Vicky knit her forehead. One thing she had got to remember was that though she must be available immediately if wanted, none the less, she must be completely unobtrusive when there were guests about. It was all very difficult for a girl who was used to having people consider her feelings rather than the other way round.

But there was one thing that she did not take into consideration. Sybil, although she had already decided she did not like the arrangement in the least, had no intention of making that clear. She was confident, Vicky's background having been what it had, that the connection would probably come to a sudden and violent end. Fergus was too used to having his own way and so was Vicky. But failing that, there were many oblique attacks that could be made, any of which was preferable to a direct one. For the time being, she intended to show nothing but friendliness towards Vicky. And that, Sybil thought with satisfaction, was where her training as a business woman came in handy. One learned to deal with infuriatingly troublesome clients with a smile on one's lips even if there were murder in one's heart.

But although Sybil was quite sure of her own self-control when she met Vicky, she had sufficient curiosity to want that meeting to occur as soon as possible, and it was her suggestion that instead of staying late in town, they should go straight to Hawthornden as soon as they had finished their day's work.

It struck Sybil that Fergus was more than usually silent on the run down, but the seven or eight miles of their journey were over too quickly to afford an opportunity of working tactfully up to a point where she could ask him what was the matter. None the less, she caught the note of relief in his voice when, on reaching the house, he remarked:

"Here we are!" and jumped quickly out of the car.

Thoughtfully Sybil remembered that Fergus had really rather leapt at her suggestion that they should not linger in Lenster. Her eyes narrowed slightly as he helped her out of the car. Yes, she must certainly be very watchful. Fergus would not be the first man who had begun by being irritated with a girl considerably younger than himself and ended by falling in love with her. It would be interesting to see what Vicky's attitude towards him was.

She went into the house with her arms full of delicate pink rosebuds, knowing that however easily an invalid can afford to buy flowers for herself, a gift is none the less delightful. She laid them gently in Mrs. Imray's arms as she bent over to kiss her, and the older woman lifted them to smell.

"Exquisite!" she murmured. Gently she caressed a petal with one of her twisted fingers, and instantly a frown creased Fergus's forehead. The comparison between the perfection of the flowers and those tragic fingers was too blatant.

"Vicky!" he called over his shoulder, and she came in instantly from the inner room. "Put these in water, will you?"

"Certainly," Vicky murmured, careful not to look at Sybil.

"Wait a minute!" Fergus went on rather curtly. "Sybil, this is Vicky Pallant who is looking after Mother. Vicky, Miss Allandyne."

Sybil was quick to see the flash that sprang up in Vicky's eyes and was quickly veiled.

"She's furious with him for making such an introduction! And he is rather a fool to have done it! It wouldn't have hurt him to call her Miss Pallant, whatever he calls her himself, just for the occasion. After all, she is at the age where dignity matters so very much!"

She held out her hand and Vicky, after a moment's hesitation, laid hers in it.

"How do you do, Miss Pallant?" Sybil murmured conventionally and Vicky, equally conventional, replied. It was a meeting of social equals and one which, quite frankly, made Mrs. Imray open her eyes. She was very fond of Sybil but far from blind to her failings, and she had frankly not expected such tact.

It was a quiet, uneventful evening. With two other people to keep the invalid company, it was obvious that Vicky need not be there all the time, and while Sybil was talking to Mrs. Imray, Vicky took the opportunity of saying very quietly to Fergus:

"I have one or two little jobs I want to do. If you need me, will you ring? I shall be in the kitchen with Maggie."

Fergus's frown deepened.

"There is no need for you to go and sit in the kitchen because we have a visitor," he said as quietly.

Vicky looked at him with limpid eyes.

"Oh, it isn't that!" she informed him. "It is just that I want to press the dress I am going to wear tomorrow evening. If you remember, I am going out!"

Fergus nodded without speaking, and Vicky left the room with the pleasurable feeling that she had got one up on him for that introduction — though for the life of her she was not really sure how she had done it!

Saturday, though cold, was a beautiful clear day, and Sybil came down to breakfast in tweeds that were at the same time entirely suitable for country wear and yet very much smarter than most women's tweeds contrived to be.

Vicky looked at her with considerable interest. It was perfectly clear that Sybil knew her own limitations. The suit was obviously man-tailored, though the choice of colour was equally obviously Sybil's. Nor could the blue-green Lovat have been better chosen. It emphasised the changing colour of her eyes, and while it served as a perfect background for her glowing skin, did nothing to take the colour from her hair. Clever, Vicky thought, but without envy. It wasn't her style in the least, and when her trunks came over from Switzerland, which they should do before long, she would have equally well-chosen clothes. Though, she realised with a sudden qualm, they would be the last clothes of that quality that she would be able to afford. She would have to take great care of them.

Shortly after breakfast Fergus took Sybil out for a tramp which would take them until lunch-time, and Vicky, with an unconsciously yearning look in the direction of the out-of-doors world and freedom, got on with her work.

It was usually Maggie's task to do Mrs. Imray's room, since the two young girls who came up daily from the village were all too much inclined to slam about with their brooms and brushes and jolt the invalid. But today Maggie had admitted, for the first time in anyone's memory, that she had a bit of a headache, and Vicky had volunteered to take on the job.

Mrs. Imray, watching her, found herself wondering just what was going on inside that pretty head. She would have liked to ask, but she realised, with a consideration shown by few employers, that to a young girl like Vicky, living in someone else's house, the lack of privacy must be a real strain. At least she must be allowed to keep her thoughts to herself. But there was a little smile curving the soft young lips that said clearly how pleasant her thoughts were, which, in the circumstances, was rather strange — in Mrs. Imray's experience it could mean only one thing. The child was in love — or falling in love. That would be an experience which would outweigh any other which had already come to her. Alice Imray's face grew thoughtful. She remembered that she had asked Fergus if there was any prospect of Vicky getting married and remembered, too, that he had said that there was nothing of the sort, so far as he knew. Yet there had been that telephone call —

Vicky was thinking of the evening to come but, if she had stopped to analyse her feelings, it was less because she was going out with Gil than because, for a few blessed hours, she was going to be free of duty or responsibility — free and frivolous! She went about her tasks with a song on her lips, and when the little masseuse from the village paid her daily visit she commented on Vicky's appearance.

"You look as if someone had left you a million!"

Vicky laughed.

"No such luck!" she said regretfully.

"Oh, well, then, you're going out with the boy friend!" the other girl insisted.

Vicky laughed again. It so perfectly described Gil. The boy friend! Neither staid nor romantic. Just a good chum and young, young, young, as she was herself!

A few minutes before half-past five, Vicky ran down the gravel drive, all agog for an evening's fun, and there was Gil. He was standing smoking beside a small car, and he pitched the cigarette away as soon as he saw her.

"A girl that turns up on time!" he said admiringly. "You're a marvel, Vicky!"

"I've learned what it means to *have* to do things to time because people pay you to. It would be strange if I wasn't punctual when I am going to enjoy myself!" she said.

"Something in that!" Gil agreed. "Well, hop in! Not exactly Cinderella's coach, but it will get us there — and back! Which is something."

Gil was by nature if not a reckless driver at least an adventurous one, but tonight he was taking no chances. Something in the way Vicky had trusted him had touched him rather more than he had thought she would have the power to do. Now, as he glanced down at her young, eager face, he found himself wondering for the first time what was going to be the outcome of this unexpected friendship that had grown up so swiftly between them.

Gil Packard had no illusions about himself. He ran his life by what was a pretty good code, but none the less he intended to get all the fun out of it that he could so long as he hurt no one doing it. His first reaction towards Vicky had been one of admiration for her performance on Buck. His second, a genuinely warm and generous desire to help the poor kid who was so obviously down in the mouth. That generosity still lingered. The last thing he wanted to do was to hurt Vicky.

He stole another look at her. Vicky was giving all her attention to the road ahead. Not, he realised, because she was a nervous type who did not trust the driver, but in sheer anticipation of the evening's fun. She would enjoy his company — he would see to that — she would share the fun. But after, it would be the way in which she had spent the evening, not the person with whom she had spent it, that would linger in her mind.

Gil faced the truth wryly. There was infinitely

less chance that Vicky would get hurt than that he himself would!

Vicky, realising how silent they were, turned inquiringly to him and smiled.

And Gil, suddenly sure of himself, smiled in return.

"Who has the child gone out with?" Sybil asked casually, putting down a piece of tapestry to re-thread her needle.

"I've no idea," Mrs. Imray admitted. "You know how young people love to keep their secrets to themselves — in any case, I've only known her such a short time that I couldn't really ask."

"No, I suppose not," Sybil admitted. "And yet, she strikes one as being such a child that it is impossible not to feel that, however unreasonably, one is responsible for her well-being."

Fergus, who had been reading, had put down his book as soon as Sybil had asked her question.

"That's rather sweet of you, Sybil," he said with obvious approval. "I can't tell you for certain, but I rather think it is a young man named Pickard who is almost a neighbour of ours, isn't he, Mother?"

"Well, darling, not exactly. His uncle, Sir Giles Tenby, lives just the other side of the valley. He calls to have a chat with me sometimes. This boy has had rather a hard time, and Sir Giles is genuinely worried because there is so little that he can afford to do to help him. However, fortunately, the boy is determined to stand on his own feet without making a fuss about it. He is in a bank and I gather that, although he does not realise it, there are several people, friends of Sir Giles' and of Gil's father, who are keeping an eye on him. He will get on, eventually."

"But in the meantime, he is hard up?" Sybil suggested. "You know, that's rather odd! I mean, Vicky has only just lost her money. It stands to reason that this boy couldn't have been one of the set that she went about with before. For they all had more money than sense! I — I wonder how long she has known him?"

Fergus moved restlessly in his chair, but he did not answer, and Mrs. Imray, with a quick look at him, herself replied:

"Even if it is a very new friendship, I do not think we need worry. From what Sir Giles says, he is a very decent boy — and, besides, Vicky has, I am convinced, standards of her own. I really don't think we need worry, Sybil!"

Sybil, subtly aware that she had lost ground, smiled and, turning directly to Mrs. Imray, answered her in a confidential way that contrived to leave Fergus out of it.

"That's splendid!" she said cordially. "Because, after all, one really can't think of anything that would help little Vicky so much as to have a good friend of her own age who will understand her problems. Of course, men don't always realise how much that sort of thing counts, but don't you agree with me, Cousin Alice?"

This time Mrs. Imray carefully avoided looking in Fergus's direction, although she was very conscious that he was listening intently.

"Yes, I think probably it will do Vicky a lot of good," she admitted. "But whether it will lead to a romance or not, I would hesitate to say. One cannot with young people of that age. But, as I have said, I am quite sure no harm will come of it, and that is the really important thing!"

"Of course," Sybil agreed. "What do you think, Fergus?"

But Fergus laughed and shook his head.

"Oh, no, you don't inveigle me into giving an opinion! As a mere man, I confess myself completely ignorant when it comes to predicting the course of a love affair — particularly with someone as unpredictable as Vicky!"

"But she is not unpredictable!" Sybil insisted quickly. "She is running completely true to form! Up one minute, down the next, resilient as a balloon and as easily deflated! That's what it means to be young, Fergus!"

"Then I think I am rather glad that I have got beyond that stage!" he said briefly, and dropped the subject as if it no longer interested him.

CHAPTER SIX

GIL brought Vicky back just after midnight after an evening which they had both enjoyed with all the fervour of youth. He had taken her to a roadhouse where they had eaten a large meal and had danced hard all the time that they were not eating. Gil danced well and so did Vicky, and the exhilaration of such an evening had gone to her head. Now it was over, which was sad, but there was the prospect of other evenings; if not so expensive, still just as much fun.

He brought her right up to the door, although Vicky had insisted that the car should be left at the gates.

"Mrs. Imray doesn't sleep very well," she explained, and Gil, though he privately thought that Vicky was worrying a lot too much about people who were really almost strangers to her, did not argue about it. That was the way that little Vicky wanted it and it was good enough for him. He, too, was in an elated mood and as they reached the front door he pulled her gently to him.

"Wait a minute, Vicky!" he said urgently, and when she turned and smiled up at him in the moonlight he caught her closer. "Kiss me, Vicky!"

He felt her stiffen in his arms, and a muttered apology was on his lips when, impulsively, she threw her arms round his neck.

"Of course, Gil!" she said warmly, and kissed him with the grateful spontaneity of a child who has been given a treat. And that was just the way Vicky did feel. Darling Gil, to have given her such a good time and cheered her up when she needed it so much!

An then, with a little gasp, she drew back. Silently the door had been opened and they stood in the flood of light from within. Fergus stood there, and though the light was behind him, Vicky could see that his face was stiff and set. Evidently he disapproved of finding his mother's companion in the arms of a young man and, worse still, just being kissed. And, with one of those swift transitions so typical of Vicky, she found that, infuriating though it was, she agreed with him. But to agree with him and to admit it were two very different things. For one thing what she did was no business of his. Nor had he any right to confuse her and try to put her in the wrong. With a desperate effort to put the situation on a conventional and less embarrassing footing, she said a little breathlessly:

"Mr. Imray, I do not think you have met Mr. Pickard, the nephew of your neighbour, Sir Giles Tenby. Gil, Mr. Imray, my — my employer."

The moment the last two words left her lips she knew that she had made a mistake. A conventional introduction implied social equality, and to appear ignorant of the fact gave the impression that she was too young and too inexperienced to know it. Tears suddenly stung her eyes. She had been happy with Gil, but the moment Fergus appeared on the scene everything was spoilt.

However, Fergus, if he noticed her *gaffe,* ignored it. He shook hands with Gil and said pleasantly:

"No, we haven't met before although, of course, I have heard of you both from my mother and your uncle. Won't you come in?"

But, unaccountably as it seemed to Vicky, Gil was suddenly ill at ease and he almost stammered his reply.

"Thanks awfully, but I'd better not. I've left the car at your gates and I'm not too sure of the battery. Besides, it's late —"

"Another time," Fergus said easily, and stood on one side to allow Vicky to pass.

A little defiantly she turned to Gil and said warmly:

"Thank you for a perfectly marvellous evening, Gil!" before hurrying into the house. As she reached the foot of the stairs she heard the door close behind her, and something prompted her to turn. Fergus was standing just a few feet away and something in his expression made her say, half defiantly, half apologetically:

"Thank you for staying up for me — but really you didn't have to, Mr. Imray! I'm quite used to coming in late, you know."

"I don't doubt it," he said unsmilingly. "But — with your permission, I will decide for myself at what time I go to bed in my own home. I, too, am quite used to being up late, Vicky!"

She looked at him uncomprehendingly for a moment, and then a wave of colour slowly mounted her face. He had completely misunderstood her, assuming that she was trying to give orders, and to him of all people! She opened her lips to explain just what she had meant, but realising that it was impossible to explain anything to someone who seemed to misunderstand deliberately, she changed her mind and without another word began to go slowly upstairs.

She had almost reached the top of the flight when she heard Fergus say:

"Vicky!" and against her will she turned.

He was standing at the foot of the stairs now, one arm resting on the newel post.

"Yes, Mr. Imray?" she said distantly.

"I like your friend. He is a good type. Decent and kind. You will be quite safe with him."

Vicky surprised at hearing Fergus refer to Gil in almost the exact terms that Gil had used about Fergus, made no reply. For one thing, what was there that she could say? And for another, she had a feeling that Fergus still had something to say. She was quite right. After a few seconds he said slowly:

"Be careful you don't take advantage of his kindness, Vicky!"

And, turning on his heel, walked back to his study, closing the door after him before Vicky realised what was happening.

When Mrs. Imray asked her the next morning whether she had enjoyed herself, Vicky answered rather soberly:

"Yes, very much, Mrs. Imray."

Mrs. Imray smiled up into the serious young face.

"I'm glad," she said warmly. "It was just what you needed. You are too young to be cooped up with a selfish old invalid without an opportunity of spreading your wings!"

"You aren't selfish," Vicky said quickly. "But — Mrs. Imray —"

"Yes, Vicky?" It was very obvious that a confidence was coming, and Mrs. Imray was careful not to let more than a very little of the deep interest that she felt show in either her voice or her expression.

"Mrs. Imray, do you think it is wrong for me to go out and — enjoy myself — so soon?" Vicky asked in a troubled voice.

Alice Imray, deeply touched that Vicky should confide in someone who was, after all, little more than a stranger, answered unhesitatingly.

"No, Vicky, I don't," she said positively. "You are young and most of your life lies before you. It would be wrong if you were to allow the mistakes of the past to overshadow you. Wrong and foolish, because you can do nothing to undo those mistakes."

Vicky sighed, and Mrs. Imray said gently:

"What has made you worry like this, Vicky? I had been hoping that you had got over the first shock of what happened."

"I suppose I have, in a way," Vicky admitted.

"Well, then?"

"Oh —" Vicky's slim shoulders moved restlessly. "Somehow — last night, I felt that Mr. Imray disapproved —"

"Of young Mr. Pickard?" Mrs. Imray asked, her eyes very intent on the downbent face.

"Oh, no," Vicky said quickly. "He said that Gil was a good type and that I should be safe with him — no, I felt he disapproved of me for going out at all. There are such a lot of things he disapproves of," she ended with a sigh.

Mrs. Imray's blue eyes twinkled.

"Well, be honest, Vicky, aren't there a lot of

things about Fergus of which you disapprove?"

"Yes, there are!" Vicky said without stopping to think to whom she was speaking. "I don't think he gets nearly enough fun out of life —"

The light in Mrs. Imray's eyes faded.

"You are quite right, Vicky," she said in a tired, unhappy voice. "Fergus has never learned to play just as, perhaps, you have never learned to be very serious. There is a lot that you can teach one another —"

"Oh!" Vicky said breathlessly. "But I should never dare to try to teach Mr. Imray anything! Besides, he wouldn't let me!"

The lost colour did not return immediately to Mrs. Imray's face, but none the less, she smiled.

"I wouldn't be so sure of that, Vicky!"

"Oh, but I am!" Vicky said quickly. "Quite sure! What is far more likely to happen is that he will teach me to be solemn and — dull. I shall wear demure grey dresses — homespun, I expect — with neat white collars. No make-up, of course. And good sensible shoes. I shall smile all the time — the sort of earnest, unmeaning sort of smile that makes other people simply furious — and I shall say 'Yes, Mr. Imray!' and 'No, Mr. Imray!', and be an old maid for ever and ever!"

"Who is going to be an old maid for ever and ever?" asked an amused voice. "Not you, surely, Vicky?"

Vicky turned quickly. Sybil Allandyne stood just inside the door, her lips smiling but her sea-green eyes extremely alert. Just for a second it flashed into Vicky's mind to wonder exactly how long she had been standing there — and how much she had heard.

"I think it would be rather fun!" Vicky said breathlessly. "No one but oneself to please — and not being tied down to just one man's company when one went out —"

Sybil laughed.

"What fun it is to be very young! I envy you your independence, Vicky! Cousin Alice, unless you want

Vicky for anything special, can I keep you company for a little?"

"By all means, Sybil," Mrs. Imray said gently. "Vicky, dear, pull up that comfortable chair for Sybil — thank you."

As the door closed behind Vicky, Sybil drew a deep breath.

"Cousin Alice, I do hope you won't think that I am being impertinent, but — do you think that was very wise?"

Mrs. Imray regarded the lovely face thoughtfully. She had known and understood Sybil long enough to have realised that, in spite of her smiles and her pleasant manner to Vicky, she had been in a disapproving frame of mind from the moment that she had come into the room.

"Vicky is at the age where she needs to let off steam," she said equably. "And to whom can she do that more safely than to me? Besides, she did not know that you had come into the room, Sybil, any more than I did. Otherwise we should probably both have been more discreet."

Her voice could not have been more gentle, but Sybil felt the reproof and flushed angrily. But she did not give in as easily as that.

"I don't think you realise just how much bother Vicky has been to Fergus," she said rather stiffly. "But he has taken me into his confidence and — I cannot help feeling that to encourage Vicky to be both rebellious and rude is hardly fair after all the trouble that he has taken on her behalf."

Mrs. Imray was silent. Quite unintentionally, no doubt, Sybil had told her two things that gave her no pleasure at all to know. First, that she resented the confidence and understanding that had always existed between Fergus and his mother. And, secondly, that she resented as much or more all that Fergus had undoubtedly done for Vicky. And neither showed a very generous nature.

"And Fergus, whatever he thinks, needs someone generous and warm-hearted," she thought, her heart contracting with love. "Cold perfection will never be enough for him!"

Vicky was not very much in evidence for the rest of the day, but when Fergus was having a last good-night talk to his mother after she had gone to bed, Sybil sought her out.

"My dear, I just wanted to have a word with you about Cousin Alice," she said pleasantly. "To begin with, I do want to congratulate you on the way in which you have cheered her up. She looks quite a different person from the one I saw the last time I was here!"

"I'm glad you think she looks better," Vicky said gravely. "I like her so very much that it seems dreadful there is so little that one can do for her."

"I know," Sybil said with a sigh. "It has worried me very much indeed that I cannot get down here more often — at least, not at present. By and by, of course —" she stopped abruptly.

Vicky looked at her quickly. So Maggie had been wrong in thinking that nothing was settled between Sybil and Fergus. Quite evidently, although she wore no ring, there was a definite understanding between them, though judging by the way Sybil had cut short what she was saying, they had decided not to make it public yet. Well, that was their business, Vicky decided.

"In the meantime," Sybil went on, "I want you to remember that if — you should need any help un-expectedly and Fergus is out of reach, you can always get me. Here is one of my cards. It is the same number both for the shop and my flat. Now, promise, Vicky! It will be a load off my mind if you do!"

"There is Maggie," Vicky said as she took the card almost reluctantly from Sybil's perfectly mani-cured fingers.

"I know. But Maggie is old — and rather worry-ingly sure that she knows best! No, I shall feel much easier —"

"The day I came here, Mr. Imray described her

91

as the mainstay of the house and their very good friend," Vicky said slowly.

"And so she is," Sybil agreed heartily, though inwardly she was becoming increasingly impatient with Vicky's apparent reluctance to accept her as one of the family. "But — she is getting older and it isn't fair to her to expect her to take too much responsibility. Don't you realise that there you have one of Fergus's chief reasons for wanting a younger person here?"

Vicky was silent, still aware of a feeling of mistrust for Sybil and yet equally aware that there must be a lot of truth in what she was saying.

Suddenly Sybil sighed and smiled at the same time.

"Oh, Vicky, I could be furious with Fergus for getting hold of you before I had a chance to!" she said with something like amused exasperation. "You would have been perfect to model some of the younger clothes I am getting out for the spring!"

"I didn't know you did the younger type of clothes," Vicky said, interested in spite of herself. "That's why I never came to you."

"I didn't until very recently," Sybil said with an air of candour. "But you know how difficult things are now. One cannot let any chance for making money go by, and by catering for the slightly older woman I have been missing all the bridal and trousseau custom."

"I see," Vicky said politely. "But — I'm afraid I can't come. I've rather promised to stay here — for a time at any rate."

"My dear child, but I wasn't suggesting that you should!" Sybil said quickly. "Please don't for a moment imagine that! Why, it would be terribly disloyal to Cousin Alice and Fergus! But that does not alter the fact that I wish I had got in first! You have a lovely figure, Vicky, and if you are not conventionally pretty, you have a very attractive, vivacious little face! Still, never mind that now! To return to the other matter. You will let me know if — anything happens?"

"Very well," Vicky said, and wondered why it was that she agreed so reluctantly to what was, after all, a very natural request.

Sybil and Fergus left for Lenster after an early breakfast on Monday morning which Vicky shared with them. It would have been rather a silent and perhaps embarrassing meal if it had not been for Sybil. She did not attempt to make Fergus talk, but kept up a conversation with Vicky which necessitated replies, however brief. It was mainly about the shop, and Sybil, evidently quite in earnest about catering for the younger women, was, as she gaily said, stealing Vicky's brains, since hers was the outlook of just the type of girl she wanted to attract.

"You'll find I am quite remorseless where the shop is concerned," she told Vicky. "I take advantage of all my friends' ideas, and the odd thing is they are tremendously flattered if I really make use of one of their suggestions, and never seem to expect that I should pay them!"

"More fools they," Fergus suddenly interjected from behind his paper, showing that evidently he had been taking more notice of the conversation than had been apparent. "Vicky, don't you give her another tip without demanding a commission! She can well afford to pay it — and don't deny it, Sybil! Remember I look after your income tax!"

Sybil laughed and pouted protestingly, but inwardly she was seething. It gave her an uncomfortable sensation of having been spied on that Fergus had been listening all the time, but there was nothing that she could do about it. Already she was beginning to realise that the undoubted streak of obstinacy in Fergus's make-up was something to be reckoned with. With a pig-headedness for which there really seemed to be no particular reason he had made up his mind that Vicky needed both looking after and training and had taken on the job himself. It was pretty obvious that nothing would deflect him from that course until he was satisfied with the results that he had achieved.

Or, alternatively, until Vicky rebelled effectively and permanently. Well, she had sown a few useful seeds this week-end which might further that end. At least Vicky knew now that there was another job waiting for her if she chose to give this one up. In the meantime, she, Sybil, must be patient — although that was hardly one of her virtues — satisfied, at least, that Fergus's interest in the girl was not a romantic one. But all the same, Vicky had got to go. Sybil was above all else a realist. She had deliberately set about making herself essential to Fergus in as many ways as possible. It was true that she really liked Mrs. Imray, at least as much as it was possible for her to like any other woman, but much of the thought and care she lavished on the invalid were given because she realised both the practical and the sentimental appeal that such an attitude would make to Fergus. Now he had introduced this girl into his home and Cousin Alice seemed to have taken to her to a quite exaggerated extent.

Deep in her own thoughts, Sybil had become temporarily oblivious to what was going on about her, and it was with a start that she came back to earth to hear Fergus saying:

"I shall be home in time for lunch on Tuesday, Vicky. Can you be ready to start immediately afterwards?"

"Certainly," Vicky murmured, and Sybil's sharp eyes saw that she was careful not to look at Fergus as she replied. So evidently there was no suggestion of a pleasure trip about whatever it was they were going to do together. None the less, it irritated her that some plan had been made of which she knew nothing. She made up her mind that she would find out what it was all about just as soon as possible, and after they had been on their way back to Lenster no more than a few minutes she said, thoughtfully:

"You know, Fergus, I've been pleasantly surprised in little Vicky."

"Oh?" he said non-committally.

"Yes. From what both you and other people had

said. I had imagined her a far more flighty young person than she appears to be. She is very good with Cousin Alice, too — though I still think it is rather unfair to so young a girl to be constantly associated with illness, even though she has an occasional break from it."

"They take girls as young as Vicky to start their training as nurses," he pointed out, his eyes intent on the road before them.

"Yes — but girls who have taken up the work voluntarily," Sybil said quickly. "You can hardly say that Vicky has done that."

"It will do her no harm," Fergus said shortly.

He was infuriatingly uncommunicative! She felt almost as if she were being physically held at arm's length, and she made up her mind that she must get through the barrier there and then before it became any stronger. She laid her hand gently on his arm.

"Fergus, no one appreciates more than I do how much you are doing for a girl who has absolutely no claim at all upon you, but — please believe me when I say that, from a woman's point of view, you are going to work the wrong way! You are too hard on Vicky, and you will breed nothing but resentment instead of the compliance you want to see in her! Oh, don't think that I mean you are being unkind to her — at least, not deliberately, but — Vicky is not used to the hard facts of life, and I believe she would adapt herself to them more easily if you were more sympathetic — more — oh, tolerant of her disposition. She is so young, Fergus, and with the upbringing that she has had —"

"Exactly!" he said almost triumphantly. "With her upbringing — don't you see, Sybil, all her life, Vicky has had every wish granted. She has had an unfair slice of this world's treasures and pleasures. Not her fault, you will say, and of course that is true. But the inevitable result, no matter whose fault it is, is that she is already resentful that life has dealt her such a harsh blow. If she ever stopped to think before this happened, I imagine she would feel that no tragedies would ever touch her. Or if they did, there would always be someone to soften the blow. And it was not an unreasonable attitude for her to take — with her upbringing. But if it had happened that way, then Vicky would always have remained a charming but spoilt child. And there is, as you have discovered and as, I admit, I have as well, far too much good in Vicky for that to be allowed to happen. I am determined that Vicky shall grow up as she ought to. And the only way in which that can be brought about is that Vicky should shoulder the burden of her troubles. Oh, not entirely, of course! It would be inhuman to expect that. But there must be no more wrapping in cotton-wool — for her own sake."

Sybil did not reply. This attitude of Fergus's was very different from the one that he had appeared to take when he had first told her about Vicky. Then he had appeared to regard her as a naughty and troublesome child. Now — no, she could not say exactly how he regarded her. But that there was some subtle change in his outlook she knew well enough. It was rather worrying — and then she remembered Gil Pickard and cheered up. After all, it was natural that youth should appeal to youth. It was a pity that he had not got more money, but if their spontaneous friendship developed into infatuation, as it probably would, then no lack of money would deter them.

So she sighed and shrugged her shoulders a very little bit.

"You are probably quite right, Fergus," she admitted reluctantly. "Men so often are, because they are realists and we are sentimentalists! So you mustn't blame me for the way I feel!"

"I don't," he said promptly. "In fact, I am very much touched at your tenderness for Vicky. While we are making sweeping statements, I would add that very many successful business women become both hard and selfish. It is pleasant to come across one who has not!"

Just for a second his hand dropped over hers. Then it was back on the wheel again, but Sybil was satisfied. She had the very real satisfaction of knowing that she had come well out of this rather trying weekend. In one way it was infuriating that Fergus, while taking no notice whatsoever of her opinions, should none the less praise her for what he evidently felt was sheer sentimentality. But as a result of it, he had, as she was subtly aware, become conscious of her as a woman in a way that he had never done before. In the touch of his hand there had been a tenderness that it was rare for Fergus to show.

It was not until she reached her flat that she suddenly realised she had found out absolutely nothing about this mysterious trip of Fergus's and Vicky's. But by then she was sufficiently well pleased with herself and events to shrug her shoulders. Probably business — and not very pleasant business for Vicky at that!

For the whole of Monday and on Tuesday morning the prospective visit to her old home hung like a shadow over Vicky. She had been perfectly sincere in her desire to do everything that lay in her power to help pay off her father's debts, but in honesty she had to admit to herself that there had been another motive as well in her decision. To see the house where she had lived all her life, the hundred and one personal possessions both of her own and her father's that made the place into a home — that would bring back a past that had gone for ever. It would be tormenting herself with memories that were better forgotten — if ever one could forget.

She recognised the fact that Fergus had no choice but to ask her help in sorting out her possessions from her father's, but she wished that it was anyone but he who would be there. There was a streak of almost obstinate courage about Vicky which she had certainly not inherited from her father and which would stand her in good stead for what must be an ordeal, but suppose it was not strong enough. Suppose she were to break down in front of Fergus. It would be humiliating — unthinkable.

So, when Fergus arrived at lunch-time on Tuesday, he was met by a girl who had relied far more on make-up than she usually did to hide the fact that her natural colour seemed to have faded completely from her face. He made no comment about either that or the fact that Vicky ate little or no lunch.

It was a very silent trip that they made to Mount View, and Vicky sat staring straight ahead, apparently completely uninterested in what must have been a familiar scene to her. To her relief Fergus showed no inclination to talk either, but as they passed through the gates leading to the house, he said, matter-of-factly:

"Manting and Mrs. Manting have stayed on as caretakers. But there is no need for you to see them if you do not wish to."

Vicky chose to accept the remark as a challenge. And instantly she took it up. Not for a moment was she going to allow him to imagine she was shrinking at the thought of meeting the butler and housekeeper who had known her since she was a little child.

"How nice!" she said promptly. "I ought really to have come and seen them, but somehow there have been other things to think about. It will be a good opportunity of assuring dear old Manty that she need not worry about me at all. She has always been rather inclined to spoil me and, of course, if you spoil anyone, you always worry about them as well."

"Both are probably the outcome of affection," Fergus commented as he stopped in front of the house.

Vicky glanced quickly at his grim, unsmiling face.

"Just like a granite mountain!" she thought, and then, flippantly, remarked: "And I am sure you feel a misplaced affection?"

"Do I?" He turned and regarded her thoughtfully. "You are in a better position to say whether that is the case than I am, Vicky! Affection is of little value to the recipient if it is unwise in its manifestation!"

"Oh, wise!" There was more than a hint of impatience in her tone. "Haven't you ever done anything loving and silly and utterly without reason or wisdom just because — just because —" She shook her head. "No, of course you haven't! You wouldn't understand that, would you? I expect it makes life very much easier for you to live by the book, but, believe me, you miss a lot of fun!"

Before he could answer, she ran up the steps and fell into the arms of the pleasantly plump woman who had evidently been watching for them, for she had opened the door just as Vicky reached it.

"Miss Vicky, Miss Vicky!" the woman crooned, stroking the smooth hair.

"Darling Manty!" Vicky sobbed, completely forgetting her determination to show no emotion in front of Fergus. "It's lovely to see you — and Manting!" She held out her hand to the butler who had quietly joined them.

"We are very glad to see you, Miss Vicky," he said earnestly. "Very glad indeed. In fact, we'd have liked to come and see you before, only we thought it might make things harder for you."

Gently Vicky released herself from Mrs. Manting's arms and glanced over her shoulder. Fergus was still standing by the car. His back was to them, and he appeared to be examining something inside the bonnet. Tact? For a moment the idea occurred to Vicky, but she dismissed it instantly. Fergus had many solid virtues, no doubt, but tact was certainly not one of them.

"I ought to have come to see you as soon as I got back," she answered. "But it was rather difficult —"

"We knew that," Mrs. Manting nodded. "But it was a great relief to know that you were in good hands. Everybody speaks well of Mr. Imray — your father thought a lot of him. And his mother is very well liked — although she doesn't have the chance of getting about and making friends, poor soul! It was good of Mr. Imray to come over to break the news to you, Miss Vicky. And to give you a home!"

"But he hasn't given me a home!" Vicky said in a high-pitched, nerve-strained voice. "I am working for him as his mother's companion! And I assure you, I certainly earn my salary!"

Neither of the Mantings replied, and in their silence Vicky suddenly realised there was a warning. She turned sharply and saw that Fergus was standing close behind her — that he must have heard every word she had said. She felt her cheeks burn, but there was nothing that she could do but ignore the fact. It was impossible to apologise and, she told herself defiantly, she had no desire to.

"Well, we'd better get on with the job, hadn't we?" she said in that same shrill voice. "I'm sure you must be wanting to get back to the office!"

"We will begin at once," Fergus said briskly. "Mrs. Manting, in about half an hour could you have a cup of tea ready for us?"

"I don't want —" Vicky began, but Mrs. Manting interrupted her eagerly.

"I've already got it laid in the small sitting-room," she announced.

Fergus nodded and turned to Vicky.

"Will you lead the way —?"

Silently Vicky went up the stairs, and inevitably she remembered the last time that she had mounted them. The car had been waiting at the door to take her to the station and she had suddenly remembered that she had left her passport, of all things, up in her room. She had run upstairs and her father, laughing and tolerant, had teased her that one of these days she would forget her own head!

"Where do you think I should be if I let my wits wander?" he had asked.

Vicky set her teeth. No use remembering. No use wishing she had never left him —

"This is — was my room," she said over her shoulder to Fergus. "There are a few odds and ends in other rooms that belong to me, but mostly they are here."

They worked steadily for twenty minutes or so, Vicky pointing out articles that could reasonably be called her personal property and Fergus carefully listing them.

Then the telephone bell rang downstairs, and Manting came up to tell Fergus that his office wanted to speak to him.

He took the call in the study. Vicky heard the door close. A minute later she slipped down the stairs herself and, avoiding both the Mantings, ran out of the house by a side door.

Half an hour later Fergus, coming in search of her, found her in the stables. Her arms were round the neck of a chestnut horse and her cheek was pressed close to its beautiful head.

CHAPTER SEVEN

AT THE sound of Fergus's step, Vicky turned sharply. He had thought as he came in that she had been crying. Now he saw that her eyes were hard and defiant, daring him to comment on the situation.

Evidently Fergus thought it best to take the hint, for all he said was:

"Mrs. Manting is ready with the tea!"

It was on the tip of Vicky's tongue to tell him that he could have tea if he wanted it, but as for herself, she would rather die than accept hospitality at the hands of the people to whom her father owed money. Then she thought of the fuss that it would mean and, shrugging her shoulders, walked past him. For a second Fergus did not follow her, and looking back she saw that he was regarding Larry, the horse that she had been fondling, with interested eyes.

"A nice little beast, that," he commented.

"Not bad," she agreed carelessly, hoping that she was being successful in hiding the love and pride that she had had for the horse that she had always ridden.

"Yours?" he asked, and saw her stiffen.

"No," she said coldly. "My father's. I rode Larry, but there was never any question of him belonging to me."

"I see," he said shortly, turning away. "Well, shall we go into the house?"

They walked back in silence, and Vicky's thoughts were not too pleasant. Why, oh why had she not insisted that Larry did belong to her? It would not have been the truth, but it would have been a lie that no one could ever have detected. And if she could have kept Larry, surely it would have been a lie that was justified. Larry had remembered her and he loved her. One owed a duty to animals who were dependent on one for happiness. Then the absurdity of the notion occurred to her. Companions with no other money than that which they earn are not able to have horses of their own. There would, surely, be few employers who would not regard it as peculiar if they were asked to provide stabling in such circumstances. Actually, at Hawthornden, there was stabling for four horses, although Fergus only kept one for himself, plus the little donkey of all work that was used in the garden. But nothing on earth would have persuaded her to ask such a favour of Fergus. No, Larry had to go.

To her relief, Mrs. Manting poured out tea for them, evidently regarding it as an opportunity for a chat with Vicky, and though that was difficult enough for Vicky with Fergus in the room, none the less, it was better than being alone with him.

Possibly Mrs. Manting thought the same thing, for several times she glanced towards Fergus; but if he realised what was in her mind, he saw fit to ignore it, and as soon as he saw that Vicky had finished he stood up.

"Now, what else is there, Vicky?" he asked briskly. "We must get through as quickly as possible, because I must go back to the office before running you home."

Little more than a half an hour saw the job completed, and then Vicky took her seat beside Fergus in the car and he set course for Lenster.

He appeared to be deep in thought, and Vicky had no desire to break across his mood. She had plenty to think of herself, and none of it was very pleasant.

Then, as they neared the town, Fergus said:

"I shall be a good half-hour. Would you like to come into the office and wait or can you amuse yourself somehow?"

"Easily," Vicky replied promptly. She had not the least idea what she would do, but anything would be better than sitting in Fergus's office, conscious of curious eyes.

"Right! Then I'll drop you just before I put her into the car park. You know where my office is, don't you?"

"Yes," she said briefly.

It was the first time that she had been in Lenster since her return from Switzerland and, as soon as Fergus left her, she looked about her curiously. Just the same, of course, since towns as old as Lenster do not change in a few short weeks, and yet, to Vicky, there was a tremendous change. In the old days, as a matter of course, she had shopped at the most exclusive shops, danced or had meals at the most expensive restaurants. Now — she had a little over three pounds left from the money that Fergus had paid her, and that was all. And it had got to last. There could be no more extravagance for Vicky. And yet, suddenly, the longing for bright lights and gaiety, for the companionship of the people she had known in the old days, got the better of her. She glanced down at her watch. There was a *thé dansant* every afternoon at Francine's. It had been the recognised meeting-place for the younger set of which she had been one, and she was particularly sure to meet someone she knew. It was only just round the corner —

As soon as she passed through the revolving doors she saw a little group of men and girls whom she knew. She saw them before they noticed her and so, when they did become aware of her, she quickly felt the sudden silence, the fading of smiles. It was only too easy to understand why. Without a falter Vicky coped with the situation. She herself smiled in a general way and waved a hand.

"Hallo!" she said brightly. "Be seeing you in a minute!"

She went over to the inquiry desk and, on the spur of the moment, invented a query. To the girl behind the desk it was purely a routine one and she answered it promptly. But that little time was enough. When she turned round, Vicky saw that the little group of her one-time friends had melted away. Vicky's heart went suddenly cold. Lance and Glenda Ingleton, her closest friends, had been among them.

She went out into the street again, and it was not

just the chilliness of the winter air that made her shiver. There were other things that could make one colder than ever the weather could. Well, she had only herself to thank. She had been a fool to imagine that anyone in that set wanted her now.

She walked slowly to Fergus's office. Her heart was crying out for the warmth of friendship, and there was no one to whom she could turn for it. Lenster became suddenly unfamiliar and frightening, and Vicky began to hurry. Suddenly she stumbled and gave a little scream as a strong hand caught her by the arm and steadied her.

"Here, what's all this?" asked a familiar voice.

It was Gil, and Vicky could have wept with joy at the sight of his pleasant, friendly face.

"Oh, Gil, I *am* glad to see you!" she said, her spirits rocketing. "Everything was *beastly!*"

"Tell me," he commanded, pulling her arm through his.

Briefly Vicky explained why she was in Lenster and what had just happened. Gil's kindly face darkened.

"Not worth worrying about!" he declared when she had finished. "Fair-weather friends never are."

"I know," she admitted. "All the same —"

"All the same, one can't get tough enough for it not to hurt." He gave her arm a little squeeze. "Never mind, Vicky, I've got a piece of news for you. Something nice!"

"Oh, what?" she asked with all the eagerness of a child.

He laughed delightedly.

"Vicky, you are a darling!" he told her. "Well — I've got tickets for the Hawthornden Hospital Ball, and you're coming to it with me!"

"Oh, Gil!" There was no mistaking the delight in her voice. Then all the sparkle died out of it. "But — suppose I can't? I mean, I did promise Mr. Imray —"

"It's on a Saturday. There's no reason in the world why you should even bother to tell him that you are going! It is the evening that he agreed to let you have, and that's that!"

"Yes, I suppose it is," Vicky agreed, and promptly forgot all about Fergus. "Isn't it fancy dress, Gil? What are you going to wear?"

"I'm going to be a soldier of the Queen!" he said, assuming a swagger and twirling an imaginary moustache. "You know, the Eton jacket and pill-box hat sort."

"Lovely!" Vicky sparkled. "You'll be a heartbreaker, Gil!"

"I wonder?" he said thoughtfully. "And you, Vicky?"

She hesitated. There was the columbine dress still stowed away in the luggage that had arrived a day or so before, but she did not feel as if she could wear that.

"I'm not quite sure, Gil. But I won't disgrace you!"

"I know that!" he told her warmly. "Well, that's a date, then!"

They had reached the entry that led to Fergus's office now, and as they stood there, Fergus himself came down the steps. He peered a little in the poor light, uncertain who it was, and then, as a passing car momentarily lit up Gil's face, he lifted a hand in greeting.

"Ah — Pickard! I didn't recognise you for the moment," he said easily and then, to Vicky: "Come, Vicky, say good-bye to your friend. We must be getting off!"

As if she were a child needing to be reminded of her manners, Vicky thought indignantly. She smiled charmingly at Gil though, unfortunately, the full effect of it was lost in the darkness.

"*Au revoir,* Gil," she said sweetly. "It is a lovely plan and I shall be looking forward to it tremendously!"

Gil, mischief in his eyes, bent formally over the hand she extended to him and kissed it softly on the wrist. It was true that Vicky was so startled she almost snatched her hand away, but that wasn't obvious enough for Fergus to see, and if, Gil thought, *he* was startled, well, so much the better! He might be, as Uncle Giles said, a decent sort, but he certainly wanted jerking out of his rut!

Vicky's thoughts on the homeward run were of Gil's invitation rather than the visit that she had paid to her old home or even of Larry, so that when Fergus said suddenly:

"I had the valuation in for your jewellery today, Vicky. It is assessed at being worth just short of a thousand pounds. Are you still determined to sell it?" she jumped, and had to collect her thoughts before she could answer him.

"My jewellery? Oh, yes, I meant it. I still do. I don't change my mind once it is made up!"

"No, I imagine not," he agreed. "But you do fully realise that no one can compel you to do this? It is a matter for you alone to decide."

"I understand," she said firmly. And then spoilt it all by adding impetuously: "I never want to see it again!"

He made no answer to that, and when he did finally speak, it was apparently about a totally different aspect of the tragedy she had experienced.

"Vicky," he said slowly, "have you ever tried to realise just what your father went through? To understand that, leaving out any question of fault, he must have been driven beyond human endurance in those few days?"

He felt rather than saw that she turned to look at him in unalloyed amazement.

"Are you — *you* making excuses for him?" she asked.

"Certainly not," he denied. "But one cannot ignore facts. It is human nature to cling to life, hard though it may be. But everyone has a breaking-point, and your father came to his. If you were to realise that — to have some pity in your heart for him instead of for yourself —"

"If you don't mind, Mr. Imray, I'd rather not discuss the matter," Vicky said distantly. "I don't think it serves any useful purpose. The past is finished —, and that is the way I want it to be. Probably you think I am very hard, but at least I never expect people to make excuses for me, so I can hardly be blamed for not making any for — other people."

Fergus did not reply, and Vicky was filled with resentment. Why was it that whenever she had managed to forget for a little, he must always remind her? Gil was right. One had to put up a barrier between the past and the present, and it always seemed that, no sooner had she laboriously built up a few more bricks than Fergus must say something that had the effect of tearing them down.

Deliberately, as soon as they reached the house, she went up to her pretty room and gave serious consideration to the question of a dress for the Hospital Ball. It was better to think of pleasant things, however trivial, than to think of the past —

She had plenty of evening dresses, but all were extremely modern and most of them strapless. There was a pale blue one, though, that she regarded thoughtfully. Its skirts were full enough to be almost a crinoline. If she wore a stiff muslin petticoat under it, it would stick out beautifully. But the top — she considered it with her head on one side. Then she gave a crow of delight. All she had to do was get a length of silk and make a fichu of it. Where it was knotted at the front she could tuck some roses, and she could stitch little rosebuds here and there over the skirt. Mittens, of course, and her silver, heel-less sandals that she had worn with the columbine dress. It would be rather fun, too, to make a poke bonnet. It would cover up her hair, which was not suitable for such a costume, and she could easily sew a few false ringlets to the bonnet itself.

"Fun!" she told herself, and ran downstairs light-heartedly.

She met Maggie at the bottom of the stairs, and the woman smiled up at her.

"Your day out has done you good, Miss Vicky!"

she said approvingly. "Master Fergus is good company, as I've always said!"

Vicky found herself smiling, because she hadn't the heart to tell Maggie that she thought Fergus was the worst of company. But the little encounter left her rather sober. It was odd, when one came to think of it, in what a variety of lights a person could appear to others. To Maggie, Fergus was good company. To his mother, the man on whom she could always rely. To Vicky herself — she grimaced expressively.

And, of course, it was the same where she was concerned. To Gil, nothing she did was wrong. To Fergus, nothing right. And yet she was the same person all the time. Or was she? Did other people's way of treating you make you really different? Or was it just that you only gave part of yourself to any other person? Perhaps that was all that you could do.

And then, dimly, it came to Vicky that the most wonderful thing in the world must be to find someone with whom you could share all of yourself — who could meet and understand you in any mood —

She shrugged her shoulders, and her lips twisted in a smile that would have been cynical if it had not been rather pathetic.

Vicky had one moment of indecision about the Ball. By chance she saw a couple of tickets for it lying on Fergus's desk. That could only mean that he was going — and probably taking Sybil. It might be awkward — then she shrugged her shoulders. After all, what did it matter? At such a big affair it might even be that she and Fergus would not see one another — particularly as they would both be in unfamiliar clothes and wearing masks. However, something prompted her to buy blonde curls to sew into the pretty poke bonnet that she had made, and there was a mischievous grin on her face when she tried it on. It made her look an entirely different person, softening her face and giving her an appealing look.

"I look as if I could swoon or have the vapours at any moment," she thought, and then carefully tucked the bonnet away in the recesses of her deep wardrobe and went about her work with a song on her lips.

Fergus, who seemed to be working at home to an increasing degree just now, came into his mother's room that afternoon and had tea with her. Vicky would have been perfectly content to have been left out of the conversation, but Mrs. Imray had ideas of her own about good manners and saw to it that she was brought into it. It was rather obvious, though, that Fergus was somewhat preoccupied, and more than once he seemed to lose all track of what was being said until Mrs. Imray gently took him to task.

"Sorry, Mother," he patted her hand. "Tell me what it was all about and you'll find I've mended my manners!"

"Nothing very important, darling," she confessed. "It was more that I wanted to distract your thoughts. You looked worried."

He laughed reassuringly.

"I shall have to watch myself! Evidently my face is too expressive!"

"But you were worrying," she persisted, and Vicky, intrigued, stole a look at Fergus. It struck her as surprising that anyone should imagine Fergus ever worried about anything. She was of the opinion that he was so sure he was always right and so equally positive that nobody would go contrary to his wishes that his life must be singularly devoid of anxieties. Consequently, now, she listened attentively to Fergus's reply.

"Not exactly worrying. Just working out an oblique attack on a problem that I cannot settle by direct means."

"And have you found a solution?" Mrs. Imray asked.

Fergus nodded.

"I think so." Then, abruptly, he changed the subject.

But at the end of the little meal he said casually to Vicky:

"If you could spare me a moment, I'd be glad of your advice — in the study?"

Vicky was so much surprised at the form of his request that her jaw dropped a little, but she followed him obediently. Fergus motioned her to a chair, but for a moment he stood silently staring into the fire. Then, abruptly, he began to speak.

"Vicky, the horses at Mount View are to be sold next week. I am thinking of buying Larry. Can you give me any idea what your father paid for him? And what his performance is like?"

Vicky jumped to her feet.

"But you can't do that!" she insisted.

He raised his fair eyebrows slightly.

"Why not? They have got to be sold. There is nothing to prevent me from bidding."

Vicky was silent. That was true enough, of course, but it seemed so pointless — unless —

"Why do you want Larry?" she demanded. "You've got a perfectly good horse yourself, and you don't ride so very much. Not enough to want another one. Besides, Larry is not the right horse for you. You would be too heavy for him."

"So I had imagined," Fergus admitted.

"Well then?"

Fergus was silent and Vicky, her suspicions not amounting to certainties, looked at him with hard, defensive eyes.

"Just because you happened to see me making a fool of myself with Larry you haven't taken it into your head to pity me, have you, Mr. Imray? Because if this is your oblique attack on a problem — if you are trying to make it possible for me to ride Larry again under the pretence that he's your horse, please don't! I don't want charity from anybody!"

"Least of all from me?" he suggested softly. "I applaud your attitude, Vicky. But has anything that has happened so far made you think that you are likely to receive charity at my hands?"

She was silent, knowing the truth of what he was

saying yet still uncertain, still not able to understand what was in his mind. And Fergus explained.

"For some time past I have been thinking of buying a horse that Sybil can ride when she is staying here. So far she has had one from the local riding stables, but that is not altogether satisfactory. Nor can I claim to have much experience when it comes to making such a purchase. Hence my desire to buy an animal which comes to me with some sort of guarantee that I am getting what I want and not being done in the process."

Sybil! That explanation was something that Vicky had not expected, but of course, it was reasonable enough. She thrust from her mind the knowledge that it would be almost unbearable to see Larry ridden by another girl, and answered shortly:

"Father gave a thousand guineas for him two years ago. He is very sweet-tempered, but he might not be too easy in inexperienced hands. It will depend on Miss Allandyne's abilities."

"I see. Well, Sybil has not ridden a great deal lately, but she has none the less had quite a lot of experience."

"If she is only going to ride Larry at week-ends, she may find him a bit fresh," Vicky said with a reluctant honesty. "You know how it is if a horse isn't worked enough — and it takes your man all his time to keep Monarch exercised."

"Quite so," Fergus said coolly. "But I shall want you to undertake Larry's exercise."

"No!" Vicky said flatly.

Fergus stared at her as if he did not believe the evidence of his ears.

"Why not? The horse needs exercising, you are a competent rider and — you can hardly claim, Vicky, that you are doing a full day's work, can you? My mother's demands do not, I am sure, over-burden you?"

Vicky was silent. Her suspicions that Fergus was making this purchase for her benefit had, perforce, been lulled. They had been aroused again by the realisation that if she agreed to what he was suggesting, she would be riding Larry five days of the week to Sybil's maximum of two. Yet now, just as she was on the point of declaring again that she would take no benefits from him, he made that impossible by suggesting that she was not doing a great deal for the money that he paid her. It flicked Vicky on the raw, and she said shortly:

"All right, I'll do it. But only on condition that you stipulate how long you want me to have Larry out and when. I don't want you turning round and saying I'm sneaking off riding when I ought to be doing other things."

"Of course, I had intended doing that." He sounded faintly surprised, as if the last thing he had thought of was to trust her, and Vicky flushed. He could always make her feel small. "That's settled, then. But there is just one other thing. I shall be glad if, next week, you can arrange to have some other evening than Saturday off. I shall have to be out then —"

"But it's the night of the Hospital Ball!" Vicky said indignantly. "No, I'm sorry, I can't give that up! You made the arrangement that I was to have Saturdays and now you'll have to stick to it!"

"Normally, yes," he agreed. "But this is an exception. You see, I am going to the Ball myself —"

"Well, why shouldn't you be the one to give it up?" Vicky demanded recklessly. "Why should it be me? And, anyhow, why did you leave it until so late? You must have known you were going —"

"I did, but, quite frankly, I forgot about it being your day off. I'm sorry, Vicky, but —"

She shrugged her shoulders.

"It hardly seems fair to me," she insisted, "that you should have both the right to dictate when I have time off, regardless of whether it suits me or not, and also the right to change your mind at the last minute! I'm sorry, Mr. Imray, but it will have to be you that stays at home!" She flung back her head, facing him defiantly. "I'm sorry if Miss Allandyne is going to be disappointed but — it's your fault, not mine!"

"It has nothing to do with Miss Allandyne," Fergus said shortly. "I could rely unhesitatingly on her understanding if it were purely a personal matter. But I happen to be on the Ball Committee, and it is essential that I should be present."

Vicky was silent, knowing that what he said was true, but not admitting it until Fergus insisted:

"You understand that it is necessary for me to be there?"

"I suppose so," she admitted grudgingly.

"Good! That's settled, then. I'm terribly sorry to disappoint you, Vicky, but — I just have no choice. We must see if there is not some other time — the New Year Dance, perhaps."

Vicky got out of the room without saying anything more. She was angry — and yet she was gleefully triumphant.

Fergus's cocksureness that nobody would dare to disobey him when he really put his foot down was enough to infuriate anybody. But that very cocksureness had led him into making a fatal mistake. He might think that Vicky had agreed to fall in with his wishes. But she hadn't. She had only said that she realised he must be present.

There was a world of difference between the two. And when Gil heard all about it, he pounced immediately on the fact.

"Of course you are coming," he insisted. "And what's more, you've told Imray that he is the one that has got to stay at home, so if he doesn't like to take the warning, well, then, it's on his head, isn't it?"

It was strange that, as soon as someone else put it into words like that, Vicky had an uncomfortable feeling that there was something specious about the argument. But Gil went on:

"It isn't as if his mother were really ill. I mean, one knows she is more or less of a cripple and in pain, but she isn't dangerously ill. If she were, neither you nor I would think of taking the law into our own hands. But as it is — now, look here, Vicky. It isn't any use arguing with people like Imray. And, in any case, if you work it the way I suggest, he'll never know a thing about it! What you've got to do is just wait until he has gone. He'll probably go fairly early as he's on the committee. Have all your things absolutely ready. Then in a little while say you've got a headache and ask Mrs. Imray if she minds your going to bed. She can't do anything but agree and then you say, please not to worry about any food or anything because you will have a couple of tablets and sleep right through. Then — you go upstairs and dress. The only risk is getting out of the house without them noticing —"

"Oh, I don't think they will. Maggie is just a shade deaf and, anyhow, there is a play they will be listening to this evening. No, that isn't what is worrying me. Suppose Fergus recognises me?"

"Do you call him Fergus?" Gil asked with interest, and Vicky shook her head impatiently.

"Of course not. It just slipped out. But — if he did recognise me —"

"He won't," Gil said easily. "Why should he? You said that you hardly recognised yourself. And he isn't expecting you to be there —"

"But it's masks off at midnight, isn't it?" Vicky asked anxiously.

Gil gave an exclamation of annoyance.

"So it is! Well, you'll have to take your choice. Either you defy him to do his worst — which is, after all, only that he should sack you. Or else be Cinderella. And, frankly, if I were you, Vicky, I'd defy him and chance it! For one thing, you've got another job up your sleeve, and for another, I don't believe he would! He's got far more to lose than you have, because he'd search a long time before finding anyone like you who would take on the job!"

"Well —" Vicky said doubtfully. "I think I'd rather be Cinderella, if you don't mind, Gil. I expect it sounds silly to you —"

"It does," he admitted frankly. "It sounds to me as if you don't want to lose your job — and that I can't for the life of me understand."

Nor could Vicky, if it came to that, so she said evasively:

"Oh, just vanity! If there is any giving notice being done, I want to be the one that does it."

"M'm," Gil said thoughtfully. "I say, Vicky, about this Miss Allandyne. He is going to marry her, I suppose?"

"Oh, yes," Vicky said confidently. "She made that quite clear and, besides, if it weren't so, he wouldn't go to the expense of buying Larry for her."

She could have bitten off her tongue as soon as she had spoken, but it was too late.

"Larry?" he asked. "This is new on me!"

Briefly she explained, ending up with:

"So you see, it must be so!"

Gil did not reply. He himself was not entirely convinced, but so long as Vicky was and, what was more, accepted the situation quite calmly, he was satisfied.

Fergus solved the question of fancy dress, a thing that few men really enjoy, by wearing Highland dress. Vicky had to admit that it became him. It is not every man who can wear the kilt to advantage, but he certainly could. The dark green of his jacket was perfect background for the jabot of lace at his throat and the ruffles at his wrists. The buckled shoes, tartan stockings and the handsome sporran he was wearing were finishing touches to a garb which he wore the more naturally because, to him, it was not fancy dress but merely one variety of the clothes that men normally wear. As a concession to the occasion he had powdered his hair, giving the impression of a wig, but that was all.

Maggie was in raptures, assuring Fergus that he was a regular heart-break and Sybil, herself an elegant figure, admitted to herself that she had as handsome an escort as any girl could want.

As for Sybil's dress, Vicky was a little bit doubtful about it. Admittedly it was lovely — a copy of an eighteenth-century ball gown in rose and gold taffeta.

116

But Vicky was pretty certain that before the evening was out Sybil would find her wide, wired skirts a nuisance — and that they would more than likely get considerably crushed. But naturally she made no comment about that, gravely congratulating Sybil on her appearance.

And then they left and Vicky's heart began to beat. Supposing it didn't work out the way she and Gil had planned — supposing — but she need not have worried. Both Mrs. Imray and Maggie applauded her good sense, and Vicky went upstairs secure in the knowledge that she would not be disturbed.

It was the work of only a few minutes to change, and with the careless confidence of youth, Vicky did not worry very much about make-up. Her own brilliant colour was enough with only the merest touch of lipstick.

She took one quick approving look at her reflection, and then she covered her pretty dress with a big black cloak.

Carefully she shut her door behind her, locked it and slipped the key into the dorothy bag that she had made to match her fichu. She knew from experience that the house was too solidly built for her to need to worry about creaking stairs, but it was a nerve-racking business all the same. At any moment a door might open and Maggie come out. But nothing of the sort happened. She gained the front door, opened it and closed it behind her, using her key to make it a silent operation.

A minute later she was flying down the gravel drive. And there was Gil waiting for her in his battered old car.

"Good-oh!" he said enthusiastically as he jumped out and helped her in. "I was beginning to get scared something had happened!"

"Not tonight," Vicky said confidently. "Nothing could! Oh, Gil, it's going to be marvellous!"

He let out a joyous toot of the horn and they were off.

The adventure had begun.

CHAPTER EIGHT

AS IT happened, Vicky had never been to a dance in the Hawthornden Assembly Rooms. Since the place was not big enough to have a Town Hall, the Rooms were attached to the local hotel, which in the old days had been a coaching inn. Most of the building was at least three hundred years old, though the Assembly Rooms themselves were an early Victorian addition. But all the periods seemed to blend in comfortably together, and it seemed to Vicky that there could not have been a better setting for such an affair. Nor could she help but know that she and Gil were as appropriately dressed as anyone there. Vicky had that reassuring feeling of melting into her background and becoming part of it. Her grey eyes sparkled like jewels through her lace-edged mask, and as they slid into the first dance, Gil gave her a quick, friendly hug.

"Something tells me that this is going to be one of those evenings!" he said exultantly, and Vicky knew that he felt the same buoyancy of heart that she herself was experiencing.

It was some time before she saw Fergus, although she was on the alert from the moment they came into the Assembly Rooms. She wished, rather uneasily, that she had seen him at once, for if she saw him suddenly and unexpectedly, it was always possible that she would give herself away by starting and calling attention to herself.

But nothing of the sort happened. Actually it was Gil who saw him first.

"Did you say kilts and powdered hair?" he whispered in her ear. "Because, if so, he's just come on to the floor. Partner is in a hooped affair — pink and gold."

"Sybil Allandyne," Vicky explained under her breath. "How's she getting on with that skirt?"

Gil watched and chuckled.

"She's looking daggers at somebody who has just

barged into her," he announced. "You can see it even through the mask! I'd take care if I were Imray! The lady may be a good-looker, but she has a nasty temper! Ever seen anything of it?"

"No," Vicky said carelessly. "Why should I? There couldn't be anyone less important in her eyes than I am."

Gil was on the verge of arguing the point, but changed his mind. In his opinion no girl engaged or nearly engaged to a man would like anyone so attractive as Vicky about the place all the time. But what did it matter to either of them if that was how Sybil felt? Least of all on this night of nights.

"Forget them!" he suggested. "There is far less chance of their spotting you if you are completely oblivious of them! I'll keep a weather eye lifted, but honestly, I don't think anyone would recognise you if they didn't know!"

It was reassuring to hear that, and Vicky realised that Gil was giving her sound advice. She threw herself heart and soul into the dancing, and more than once Gil held her away from him to smile down triumphantly into her flushed face as they successfully completed a complicated series of steps.

"You're a marvel, Vicky!" he told her. "I've never danced with anyone half so good in my life before!"

"I love it so," Vicky confessed. "I feel a different sort of person altogether! Particularly when I am dancing with someone who is good too, and enjoying it. You're marvellous, Gil!"

"Here, steady, if you say things like that, they may go to my head and I shan't be able to concentrate," he said rather shakily. "Oh, darn it, that's the end of that one!"

"What's next?" Vicky said as they went off the floor, and consulted the little card with its hanging pencil with which she had been presented on her arrival. "I think this is a lovely idea, Gil. I wish they always did it at dances. I know it's old-fashioned, but I like it!"

He looked down at her with something very tender in his blue eyes.

"Bless you, infant, you'd like anything this evening! It's an old-fashioned waltz, and take it from me, I'm going to dance you off your feet!"

He was as good as his word, and at the end of the dance, Vicky was breathless and laughing.

"Take me out somewhere to get some fresh air!" she implored him. "Goodness, Gil, our ancestors must have been tough if they could dance like that all the evening!"

Gil took her out on to a balcony, and together they watched the glittering stars in the velvet sky. At first they talked a little in undertones that seemed to suit the quietness of the night, but then they fell into a silence that Gil at least was reluctant to break lest the magic of the moment should be shattered at the same time. Yet something in him craved to know whether Vicky's silence sprang from the same cause. His arm slid round her little waist.

"Vicky, darling —" he began, but at that moment the music began again and Vicky caught his hand in hers.

"Come along!" she insisted. "We mustn't miss a moment of it!"

Gil followed her in silence, knowing now that the enchanted moment which he had experienced was something that Vicky had not shared. Otherwise she would be as reluctant as he was to go back to the bright room and the gay music.

But at the door of the ballroom, Vicky paused. "Oh — a Paul Jones!" she said doubtfully. It was really too much of a risk — but, before she could draw back, she was swept into the circle of girls and lost sight of Gil. Round and round they went and then the music stopped. Vicky drew an unconscious sigh of relief. She had no idea who her partner was, but that she knew it was not Fergus. The second time round she paired off with a red-headed Jacktar who was so obviously on top of the world that she forgave him for being quite the worst dancer she had ever encountered. He dated her up in extravagant enthusiasm for at least six more dances, adding ingenuously:

"And don't forget! So many girls seem to have the rottenest memories these days! I've had three dances cut this evening!"

A laugh trembled on Vicky's lips. Really, it was not surprising. One might endure one dance in which one's partner trod on one's feet almost every other step, but not more. And the pet was so unconscious of his shortcomings!

And the third time round, the music stopped just as she was opposite Fergus! She had seen the possibility of it as he came nearer and nearer, and there was nothing that she could do to avoid him except wish with all her heart that the music would stop either before he had reached her or after he had passed. But there could not have been any good fairies listening to Vicky, for — it stopped just as he was opposite her.

Fergus bowed with a ceremoniousness that somehow seemed in keeping with his appearance and Vicky, partly because her knees were just about giving and partly because his own manner seemed to demand it, sank almost to the ground in a graceful curtsy.

The next minute she was in his arms and they were dancing a waltz. Studiously Vicky kept her eyes lowered and wondered how on earth she could disguise her voice so that he would not recognise it. A mask and fair curls were all very well at a distance, but one's voice was a different matter.

And then she forgot all about such considerations. In Gil she had recognised an extremely good dancer, but Fergus was even better. Gil's performance had been a reflection of her own youth and exuberance, but Fergus — there was something totally different. A smoothness, a sense of security and a complete surrender to the rhythm of the music.

And, as they danced in unbroken silence, Vicky realised that this was the first time that Fergus had so much as touched her hand except by chance. Fergus could have told her that she was wrong. He had picked her up in his arms when Glenda Ingleton had blurted out the news of her father's suicide and had carried her up to her room. But Vicky knew nothing of that.

The dance came to an end and Fergus led her off the floor.

"That was delightful," he commented pleasantly. "And all the more so because, unlike most girls, you realise that conversation is an interruption to the perfect enjoyment of dancing!"

Vicky made a strangled little sound that Fergus might conceivably have taken for agreement and then, as he bowed again, she murmured "Thank you!" and hurried off as quickly as possible to the spot where she and Gil had chosen to sit during the intervals. He was waiting for her now.

"That was a narrow squeak!" he commented. "How did you get on? Did he guess?"

"He couldn't have done," Vicky replied. "Otherwise he would have said something!"

"And he didn't?"

"We hardly spoke at all," Vicky admitted. "But when he did, it was quite different from the way he usually does to me."

"Good!" Gil said rather absently, as if he had already dismissed Fergus from his mind as unimportant. "Well, don't let's waste any time, the music is starting again!"

"What time is it?" Vicky asked anxiously. "I simply must go just before twelve, Gil."

"Oh, that's all right," he said easily. "I'll see you get away in time! Come along!"

Obediently she went with him, but after a moment or two Gil held her away from himself and looked down into her face.

"Here, what's the matter?" he demanded. "You haven't spoken a word since we began this dance, and you're dancing as if you were in a dream! Wake up, Vicky!"

She had started at the sound of his voice, and now she smiled reassuringly up at him.

"I expect it shook me a bit, dancing with Fergus," she excused herself. "I'm sorry, Gil!"

"Oh, that's all right!" he said, quickly mollified. "After this dance, how about getting something to eat? Otherwise you'll have to go hungry! It's after half-past eleven now!"

They went into the supper room, and though quite a lot of people had unmasked already, there were sufficient still masked for Vicky not to attract attention.

Gil collected a trayful of food and drink and brought it to a small table where Vicky was already sitting. It was a delightful little meal and they both thoroughly enjoyed it. So much so, in fact, that neither noticed the passing of time until as a couple brushed past their table they heard the girl say:

"Well, I make it twelve already! It can't be far short anyway!"

And Gil, glancing down at his watch, gave a little whistle of surprise.

"It *is* just on twelve!" he announced. "Vicky, if you're determined not to let Imray know you've been here, you'd better scoot! Go and get your cloak while I get the car started!"

Vicky fled, but the hour had already chimed as she hurried down the stairs. Several playful hands made a grab at her mask, but she contrived to evade them. It was her friend of earlier in the evening, the Jack-tar, who was most persistent. He followed her to the door and Vicky, in her haste, tripped over her long cloak. She recovered herself quickly, but it meant an awkward placing of her foot to do so and she felt the satin ribbon of one sandal give. She dared not stop to attend to it, and as she ran, she found it impossible to keep it on her foot.

Fortunately, she had only a smooth stretch of concrete on which to walk to the spot where Gil was waiting for her, and though it was cold, she managed it quite easily.

"That was a nearly!" Gil commented as he let in the clutch. "Nobody saw your face, did they?"

"No," she said breathlessly. "I lost a shoe, though!"

Gil chuckled.

"Genuine Cinderella stuff!" he said. "Well, I'll simply have to run you right up to the house now. You can't walk up that gravel drive without a shoe."

"Oh, yes, I can manage," she insisted. "Truly, Gil! I can walk on the grass! It would give the whole game away if you were to take me right back."

"Well —" He seemed doubtful, but eventually he agreed and set Vicky down at the gates. He watched her until she vanished into the shadows. Then he sat there for a moment, undecided what to do. Suddenly he realised that another car was coming up behind him and discreetly he started up himself and slid off. Then something occurred to him. The other car had slowed down. He could tell that from the sound it made. He looked into his driving mirror and saw to his horror that his suspicions were correct.

The car had slowed because it wanted to turn into the gates at which he had just left Vicky. And, in the moonlight, he recognised it as Fergus's car!

He whistled softly.

Coincidence that Fergus should also have returned early? It took a bit of believing!

Then Vicky was for it — and there was not a thing he could do about it.

Vicky had really thought that it would be possible to run up to the house mainly across grass, but what she had forgotten was that the grass was intersected at intervals with garden beds, and after she had tripped up over one and scratched herself rather badly on a leafless rose bush, she saw that the only thing for it was to walk on the gravel, even if it did hurt her feet.

And it did hurt. Very badly. Especially the one that had lost its shoe. More than once she only just suppressed a little cry of pain, and when at last she reached the front door, she had to pause for a moment to get her breath back. Then, cautiously, she let herself in and as silently shut the door.

There was no sound in the house, and though the hall and landing lights were on, she knew that it was simply for Fergus's and Sybil's benefit and was careful not to turn them out. It was when she had reached the turn in the staircase that she grew suddenly frightened.

Up the drive swept the powerful headlights of a car, and reason told her that, at that time, it could only be Fergus. Of course, he might have come home for some perfectly ordinary reason totally unconnected with her, but she was taking no chances. She did not dare to switch on the light in her room, but she cautiously drew back her curtains to take advantage of the moonlight. Then, hastily, she tore her dress off and thrust it under her bed. Her stiff petticoat followed suit and the solitary sandal last of all.

Then she jumped into bed and sat there shivering with cold and suspense. She heard the front door being quietly opened and then firm if careful footsteps coming up the stairs. She held her breath. If Fergus had come home for something he had forgotten, then he would probably be going to his own room and he would turn left at the top of the stairs and the sound of his steps would fade away. But if he had recognised her —

Her heart gave a great leap. He had turned to the right — towards her room. And a moment later there was a quiet tap at her door. She did not answer then or when the sound was repeated. And then Fergus's voice, unmistakably peremptory, said:

"Vicky, I want to speak to you at once! Do you hear me?"

Even if she had been asleep, it would be impossible for her to pretend that she had not heard him then, and in a muffled voice as if she had just been roused she said:

"What is it? What's wrong?"

"Come here at once, please," Fergus said sternly, and Vicky knew that she had to obey.

She switched on her light, put on her dressing-gown and thrust her feet into bedroom slippers. Her torn foot made her grimace with pain, but she managed to shuffle to the door and open it.

Fergus was standing there, and one look at his face made her eyes drop.

"Let me see your foot," he demanded, and at that her last hope of escaping detection vanished.

"I don't —" she began.

Without troubling to argue, Fergus dropped on one knee and forcibly lifted her foot. He pulled the bedroom slipper off it and turned her foot so that the light shone on it.

"Will you never learn sense, Vicky?" he asked in evident exasperation and then, before she could answer or protest, he swung her up in his arms and began to carry her down the corridor.

"Put me down!" she demanded in a voice that was no less urgent because it was muted. "Put me down!"

But though she struggled, he took no notice except to tighten his grip on her so that she could not break loose. At the top of the stairs he halted.

"You'd better keep still," he told her grimly. "Because I have every intention of taking you downstairs, and if you struggle like that you will quite likely bring both of us down."

How could one fight such obstinacy as that? Suddenly Vicky knew that she could not, and she lay still in his arms.

"That's better!" he commented, and began to descend the stairs.

He carried her without hesitation, as if he had already made up his mind just what to do, out to Maggie's kitchen, and set her down in the basket chair.

"Keep your foot off the floor," he ordered, and went to the outer kitchen where Vicky could already hear a kettle singing. Evidently Fergus had put it on before he had come up to her — in fact that was obvious, for on the kitchen table lay her silver sandal. With a little gasp she remembered that she had worn them that night in Switzerland and, of course, he must have recognised them.

In a moment or two he came back with a basin of warm water and set it on the floor. What he intended doing was obvious.

"No!" Vicky protested. "No — you can't —"

Fergus took no notice. He went to a cupboard that was evidently Maggie's first-aid store and took out a bottle of disinfectant and a piece of lint. He added some of the disinfectant to the water in the basin and soaked the lint in it. Then he knelt down in front of Vicky and held out his hand. She hesitated. It seemed so incongruous that Fergus, of all people, should be doing such a thing for her.

"At once, Vicky!" he said quietly, and Vicky lifted her foot so that he could hold it firmly while he bathed it.

His touch was firm but astonishingly gentle, and gradually Vicky's taut little body relaxed. She lay back against Maggie's rainbow of cushions and her eyes rested wonderingly on Fergus's bent head.

Suddenly he looked up and though he did not speak, Vicky crimsoned. Then he returned to his task, and at last he appeared to be satisfied that the foot was really clean. He dried it carefully on another piece of lint, spread some ointment thinly over the injured parts and bound the whole foot up.

"There, that ought to do!" he commented, standing up.

"Thank you!" Vicky murmured. "It — it is much comfier!"

Fergus glanced at her, but he did not speak until he had cleared away the basin and tidied the disinfectant and the remainder of the bandages into the cupboard.

He seemed a little uncertain then just what to do, and Vicky shrank back in her chair. He had not uttered a word of reproach until he had cared for her injuries, but that could not be deferred now, and Vicky's conscience told her that she deserved everything that was coming to her.

Suddenly, as if he had at last made up his mind, Fergus drew up a wheelback chair in front of the fire and sat down in it. But even then he did not speak immediately. His hands clasped loosely between his knees, he leaned forward looking into the fire, and he was still in this position when he said, abruptly:

"Vicky, I owe you an apology!"

It was the last thing that she had expected him to say, and involuntarily she gave a little gasp. He swung round and regarded her thoughtfully.

"Yes, decidedly," he commented, as if he were confirming his own amazing statement. "I should have trusted you more!"

"Trusted me?" Vicky gasped. "But —"

Fergus stretched out his hand and took hers firmly in it.

"Vicky, why did you think I stopped you going to the Ball tonight?"

She was silent for a moment. Then she said slowly:

"Because of your mother, really, I suppose. Although —"

A crooked smile softened his harsh features.

"Although it sounded more like cussedness than anything else?" he suggested.

She darted a quick look at him and seeing the smile, herself grinned rather ruefully and nodded.

"Also, you thought I was making a lot too much fuss about an ailment that, although it is desperately painful, is unlikely to be fatal?"

"Yes," she admitted rather shamefacedly.

"Yes." He seemed to be speaking to himself rather than to her. "What else could anyone think? I blame myself — I should have trusted you, Vicky. But you see, I felt that the fewer people who knew the better."

"Knew what?" Vicky asked, alarmed at the gravity of his face.

"That, apart from her other ailments, my mother's heart is in a bad way," he explained slowly, and she saw the twitch of the mouth that, for the first time, she realised was extraordinarily sensitive.

"How bad?" she breathed, and in Fergus's silence and in the pain in his face, she realised the truth.

"Now you see why Maggie must not be left alone with her," he explained. "It may be — any time."

"Does — does Mrs. Imray know?" Vicky whispered, and Fergus shook his head.

"She has not been told, but — my mother is a difficult person to deceive."

"I think she knows," Vicky said softly. "And — I do not think she is afraid."

His grip on her hand tightened, but he did not speak, and after a while Vicky said steadily:

"You can trust me. I promise I will never let you down again!"

He turned slowly and looked at her, and she felt that his dark eyes were reading her as if she had been a book open for his inspection.

"I am grateful for that promise, Vicky!" he said softly, and lifted her hand so that he might touch it to his lips.

They sat in silence for a while, each deeply occupied with their own thoughts and yet, in Vicky's case at least, intensely conscious of the other's presence. At last Fergus sighed and stood up.

"Bed for you now, Vicky!" he said briskly. "And I must go back and put in an appearance at the Ball or they will think I am shirking my duties!"

"And — you must bring Miss Allandyne back as well," Vicky suggested.

If it had not been absurd, she could have sworn that Fergus started as if he had forgotten Sybil entirely and found her reminder timely.

"Yes, of course!" he agreed quickly. "Now then, I'm going to carry you up —"

"It isn't necessary —" she began shyly, but Fergus took no notice. He swung her up in his arms as if she were a child, and she saw that he frowned.

"What is it?" she asked, half fearfully.

"Only that I'm certain you don't weigh enough, my child," he told her. "I had not realised before —"

"Oh, I never have," she said lightly. "But Maggie

simply stuffs me now — really, it's just that I'm the skinny sort!"

He smiled, and turned to carry her out of the kitchen. Then his eyes fell on the sandal and he turned so that she could pick it up.

"If it hadn't been for my losing that —" she said ruefully.

"Oh, that!" he dismissed it as unimportant. "I knew it was you long before you lost your little shoe, Vicky!"

"Did you?" She made no effort to hide her amazement. "But how?"

He shrugged his shoulders.

"Never mind," he said shortly. "Now — upstairs!" He set her down at her door.

"Can you manage now?" he asked, and she nodded silently. "Then — good night, Vicky! Sleep well!"

She smiled but did not reply, and as she went into her room and shut the door slowly after herself, she knew that sleep would certainly not come easily.

She had far too much to think about — the information that Fergus had imparted to her, for one thing. But even more than that, her mind was full of the amazing knowledge that had come to her in the last half-hour. Even now it seemed unbelievable and yet —

She stared down entranced at the hand on which Fergus had imprinted that gentle kiss. Then slowly she lifted it and pressed her own lips to the place where his had touched.

CHAPTER NINE

GIL rang Vicky up the next morning, and although there was no one about, she found herself answering his questions with a restraint that he was quick to notice.

"Did he go for you?" he inquired aggressively. "Because if so —"

"Oh, no, no!" Vicky said hastily. "Nothing like that. It was — it was quite all right."

Gil was silent for a moment. Then he said shrewdly: "All the same, something happened, didn't it?"

"Yes," she admitted helplessly. "It did. But — I can't —"

"I know," he said quickly. "You can't tell me on the 'phone."

It was not what Vicky had been going to say. She had suddenly realised that in his anxiety for her happiness, Gil was going to present something of a problem. It was not that she did not trust him. Had it been her secret, Gil would have been one of the few people with whom she would have shared it. But the condition of his mother's health was Fergus's secret and he had trusted her not to pass on his confidence. So she could not even tell Gil. Yes, it was going to be very difficult, as his next remark showed.

"I've got to see you, Vicky!" he said flatly.

"Oh, Gil, I don't know that I can —" she began, but he interrupted her immediately.

"Look here, Vicky, either you make an opportunity to meet me in an hour's time or else I come up to the house. You can choose."

It was so unlike Gil to be assertive that Vicky was surprised into saying:

"I'll meet you — but not too near the house. In the field where I rode Buck."

"Right!" Gil agreed. "I'll meet you there —" there was a pause as he evidently glanced down at his watch "— at half-past eleven!"

It would have been easy enough for Vicky to slip away, for all her protest. Sybil was with Mrs. Imray and Fergus himself was out. He had gone over to Mount View to fetch Larry, although Vicky was ignorant of the fact.

However, in spite of the fact that her time was, for the moment at least, her own, she went to Mrs. Imray and explained that she would like to go out for a walk. Mrs. Imray agreed immediately and without question, but Sybil, lifting her eyes from the beautiful piece of needlework she had been doing, said lightly:

"Going to meet the boy friend, Vicky?"

Vicky flushed. There had been both amusement and patronage in her tone — a patronage that had suggested how very immature and unimportant she felt Vicky to be.

"No, Miss Allandyne," she said with a show of composure that would have been completely beyond her a few short weeks ago. And then, turning to the older woman: "Thank you, Mrs. Imray. I shan't be very long."

She went out of the room, and as the door closed gently behind her, Mrs. Imray turned to Sybil.

"My dear, forgive me, but I don't think you should have said that to Vicky!"

Sybil looked up in genuine surprise.

"Said what, Cousin Alice? Oh — about the boy friend! But why not? It isn't as if it were likely to be serious! If it were, I wouldn't have said anything, but at that age, a child — particularly of Vicky's type — is incapable of anything but superficial calf-love!"

"Possibly," Mrs. Imray admitted, her fine face suddenly shadowed. "But if you are right, don't you think that is all the more reason why one should be very careful? You see, young things have an uncomfortable suspicion that they are not really so grown up and sophisticated as they could wish — that is why they so often over-act the part. I think it is kinder to stand aside and accept everything they say and do as right and natural. They find their feet less painfully that way — particularly when they are as sensitive as Vicky."

"Vicky — sensitive!" Sybil laughed, and a little sadly Mrs. Imray wondered if she realised how harsh a sound it was. "That is the last word I should use to describe her!"

"Vicky has been through a great deal lately," Mrs. Imray said quietly. "And her experiences have been crowded into a very short time. It is not surprising if she has changed a great deal from the headstrong child she was."

Sybil did not reply. She was angry both with herself for calling down such a rebuke, gentle though it was, and with Mrs. Imray for delivering it. Surely Cousin Alice must realise that in this house, she, Sybil, was a privileged person and as such should not have her actions criticised. Deliberately she folded up her needlework and stood up.

"I have some letters to write, if you will excuse me, Cousin Alice," she said distantly. "Unless, of course, you would prefer not to be alone?"

"It is quite all right," Mrs. Imray said gently. "You might ask Maggie to come and see me for a moment, please."

With the unreasonable feeling that she had been dismissed, Sybil went in quest of Maggie. Nor was her temper improved by the fact that she felt she had Vicky to blame for the rebuke she had received.

Gil was already sitting on the gate when Vicky arrived, but he jumped down as soon as she came in sight.

"I thought you were never coming!" he declared, taking her hand in both of his.

"But I'm early!" she protested, wide-eyed.

Gil looked at her intently, and a little muscle at the corner of his mouth twitched. Odd that Vicky had not the least idea of his feeling for her — odd, that was, unless such a thing seemed beyond the bounds of possibility because, for her, there was somebody else.

"I've been worried," he said, and let that stand as an excuse for his impatience as, in part, it was. "What happened last night? I saw Imray's car go in at the drive, but I was afraid I would only make things worse if I came barging in."

"You would have," Vicky agreed. "Well — actually, nothing much happened," she went on carefully, aware that she had got to give Gil an explanation which would satisfy him and which, at the same time, would not betray Fergus's confidence. "Mr. Imray found my shoe —"

"How did he know it was yours?" Gil interposed sharply.

"Oh — I wore that pair the night he came to the hotel in Switzerland," she explained. "Besides, he had recognised me, anyhow."

"Had he, though?" Gil said softly. "Then why didn't he do something about it then and there?"

"I don't know," Vicky admitted. It was a question to which she had not found an answer although she had puzzled quite a lot over it. "Anyhow," she rushed on, "he came home and — and — I had gone to my room. He told me to come downstairs, so I did, and he insisted on bandaging up my foot — I had hurt it running up to the house. And — and then he asked me to promise never to let him down again like that and I said I wouldn't. And I won't either. Ever. That's all," she finished lamely.

"Is it?" Gil put his hand under her chin and turned her candid child's face up so that he could look into it. His blue eyes, more sober than was usual, searched it closely and saw — that it was no longer a child's face.

"That, Vicky, is only half the story," he said gently. "But you do not need to tell me the rest because — I know!"

"You know!" Vicky gasped. "But you can't!"

Gil laughed sadly.

"But I do!" He put a steadying arm round her shoulders. "My little Jane, you love your Rochester, don't you?"

Vicky's eyes dropped from his and she stirred restlessly in his arms. But at last she nodded.

"Only he isn't like Mr. Rochester," she protested. "Not a bit!"

"No?" Gil asked quizzically. "Then what is he like, Vicky? What makes you love him?"

Vicky was silent. It was not an easy question for her to answer for, in some inexplicable way, it was all bound up with her father and the love that there had been between them.

To her, Mark Pallant had been her guiding star. His gaiety, his optimism, his recklessness, these had seemed to Vicky the most desirable characteristics that there could be in any human. Then she had realised that her father, far from being a guiding star, had been no more than a flickering candle at the mercy of every wind that blew. And she found herself with nothing by which she could steer her life.

Then she had met Fergus. Rather scornfully she had remembered that her father had always said he was utterly honest, but dull, and she had accepted his verdict without question. But gradually she had realised that there was something more to Fergus's character than that. Of all the people who knew of her altered circumstances, he had been the only one who had done anything to help her. Even now she shrank a little when she thought of her encounter with the young Ingletons that day at Francine's. It had shown her, in sharp contrast, the difference between people like her old friends and Fergus. It was true, of course, that it had been to Gil that she had turned for immediate comfort and he had given it to her, generously and warmly.

And yet, though she had refused to listen to the warning, there was something that Gil had not got it in him to give her. It was not that he was a weakling in any sense of the word but, like her, he was young, inexperienced and living for the moment rather than to any plan of life.

Fergus — she had resented the knowledge that he was stronger than she was herself, hated him when he had forced her to set her feet on the hard but inescapable path along which her life must lie for the future. But because, however reluctantly, she had accepted the situation, something had happened to her. She had learned to stand on her own feet, no longer at the mercy of chance as her father had been. Last night's escapade had been her last tilt against responsibility, and suddenly she realised that Fergus had known that. He had not been angry with her as he would have been not so very long ago. Instead, he had first cared for her hurts and then treated her as an equal on whom he could rely. And Vicky's wayward, tender heart swelled with the knowledge that, strong though he was, Fergus should turn to her for help —

Gil, watching the changing emotions pass over her expressive little face, knew that there was no need for her to answer his question. He had thought to challenge her to prove she loved Fergus, but now he was convinced.

His heart ached with the knowledge. Since the day he had first met Vicky, not so very long ago, he had known that she would always mean something special to him but now, in spite of his heartache, he wondered whether things were not better as they were. With the uncompromising honesty of his generation he admitted to himself that there was something so elusive, so gossamer-like about what he felt for Vicky that it might not have stood up to the knocks of everyday life.

"My most perfect dream!" he thought, and smiled wryly.

But he had, unconsciously, spoken his thought aloud, and Vicky looked up at him in a troubled way. Her own wits sharpened by her newly discovered love, she could read what was behind his words.

"Oh, Gil," she said pitifully. "Please, please, don't be unhappy about me!"

It was his final *congé* and he took it gallantly.

"Bless the child!" he said, and pinched her cheek. "The conceit of it!"

Vicky smiled crookedly, very near to tears, and slipped her arms impulsively round his neck.

"I shall never forget all you've done for me," she whispered. "Oh, Gil, I do wish you were my brother! It would solve everything so beautifully!"

Gil laughed with genuine amusement and saw the corners of Vicky's mouth curve in answer.

"It's a wonderful idea, darling, but all the same, I don't wish it at all!" He bent and kissed her lightly on her soft mouth. "Remember, Vicky, if ever you need me, you know where to find me!"

And the next moment he had left her and was swinging off across the field.

Vicky stood very still for a moment, watching and regretting the friend she had lost. Then slowly she made her way back to the house.

Fergus had already returned by the time she got there, but he made no comment on her absence. In fact, he was extremely quiet for the rest of the day. So quiet that Sybil lost some of the feelings of satisfaction that Fergus's purchase of Larry had given her and wondered, rather irritably, whether the game was worth the candle. Fergus was getting duller and duller every day.

It seemed incredible to Vicky that, after such a week-end, it was possible for life to return so nearly to normal on Monday after Fergus and Sybil had gone off to Lenster. It could not, of course, be entirely normal, for two things made that impossible. One was Vicky's knowledge of the shadow that lay over the house, and the other was that she had now to redeem her promise to Fergus that she would exercise Larry.

She smiled a little wistfully to herself as she dressed for her first ride. When Fergus had first told her that he wanted her to undertake Larry's exercise she had rebelled bitterly. Now, although she knew that it was really for Sybil's benefit, it was a dear delight to carry out Fergus's request.

Larry, after having lacked much exercise for weeks, was rather fresh, but her familiar voice and compe-

137

tent hands soon put him on his best behaviour, and Vicky had more time to look about her. She was riding away from the district in which she had usually ridden in the old days, for between Mount View and Hawthornden there was a ridge of fairly high ground too closely wooded to take a horse. None the less, the countryside was much the same as that to which she was used, and she experienced an oddly reassuring sense of familiarity. She could not have explained very clearly to anyone just what she meant, but it seemed to her as if her old life and her new were in some way linked as they had not been before. Instead of feeling that there was an impassable chasm between the two she began to realise that, after all, she still was the same person that she always had been. Altered circumstances did not alter that.

Almost unconsciously she began to sing as she always had done when she was riding, and when her father had been with her he had joined in. Now, out of the past, she could hear the gay, tuneful echo in her ears and the tears stung her eyes. He had been so gay — so full of life. How could he — how could he have done what he did? Somehow now she could think past that first aching hurt to her own heart, and Fergus's words — Fergus of all people! — came into her mind: "He must have been driven beyond human endurance!"

It was true! She could believe that now. He had been distraught and, like a trapped animal, he had not known which way to turn. And not the least of his burdens would be the knowledge of her own dependence on him. Vicky's heart ached — not for herself, but for the man who had had no one to stand by him as Fergus had stood by her.

When she went back to the house half an hour later she took a spray of wild rose-hips, scarlet and polished, for Mrs. Imray. All her life Mrs. Imray had loved to spend as much time as she could in the woods and fields, and nothing gave her so much pleasure now that she could not go out as to be brought a treasure like this.

"How lovely!" she said as Vicky laid it in her hands. "Are there a lot of berries this year? It is supposed to mean a hard winter, so they say, but so far it has been very mild. Vicky, do you think you and Fergus could bring in berries and leaves for Christmas decorations when he is home next week-end?"

Vicky did not answer for a moment; then she said quietly:

"Miss Allandyne will be here. I expect Mr. Imray would like her to help him."

Maggie, who was sitting darning beside the fire, looked up sharply at the girl, but Mrs. Imray, her eyes still intent on her berries, replied easily:

"Sybil is not coming down next week-end. She is paying a visit to some cousins in the south."

"Oh!" Vicky's heart gave a wild little thump as she conjured up a mental picture of such an outing with Fergus. "I see. If Mr. Imray would like me to help him, of course I will."

As she went out of the room to change into her ordinary clothes the eyes of the two women met.

"It's no' so easy to read her thoughts as it was when she came here," Maggie commented.

"She is growing up," Mrs. Imray said gently. "And into a very sweet girl, too."

Maggie nodded as she tidied her work away.

"A girl any man should be proud to marry," she remarked, and again their eyes met. But though they understood one another very well, neither made any more comment on the subject.

On Saturday the weather which had, all the week, been growing steadily duller, suddenly turned over a new leaf. The grey skies cleared and became almost as blue as if it were spring instead of winter. The sun shone, and if there was not much warmth in its rays, it was at least cheerful and bright.

Fergus acceded to his mother's request without hesitation, and seemed to take it for granted that Vicky should come with him. So they set out in the station wagon that Fergus frequently used when he was at home, took secateurs and a pruning-knife with them and, at the last moment, a basket which Maggie suddenly appeared with.

"Food," she explained succinctly. "I know you fine, Master Fergus! The fresh air always gives you an appetite. And that's all to the good! You've no' been looking yourself for some time past. Oh, you don't deceive me!"

"I wouldn't try to, Maggie," Fergus said meekly, and then turning to Vicky: "Maggie will always have it that I am pining away, but as a matter of fact, it is sheer vanity on her part. She knows quite well that she is a good cook, but she is afraid other people won't realise it if I don't look as though I am growing out of my clothes!"

"That's not true!" Maggie protested, outraged at the suggestion. "Miss Vicky, if you'd seen what a thin wee bit of a laddie he was — all bones and beak, the doctor used to say!"

"That's a gross libel, Maggie!" It was Fergus's turn to be outraged now. "And extremely disrespectful to your employer. One of these days, I'll be giving you notice!"

"Just you try!" she suggested, obviously immensely amused at the suggestion. They exchanged a glance of affection and understanding, and Vicky watched with something like envy in her heart. This was a gay and light-hearted side of Fergus that had not showed before, and she would have given anything to have been the one who had called the mood into existence. Then she consoled herself with the knowledge that at least Fergus had not minded her witnessing his holiday mood.

And, as the day progressed, she realised that she was sharing it. He seemed to have laid aside all cares and responsibilities as he drove out to the woods, and, to Vicky's amazement, began to sing some of the songs that she had shared with her father. After a moment's hesitation she joined in, and at the end of it, they looked at one another and laughed for sheer high spirits.

He left the car as near to the wood as possible, and they began their search. There was plenty of holly, glossy and well berried. Fergus, wearing a stout pair of gardening gloves, insisted on cutting and carrying that, while Vicky devoted her attention to cutting sprays of hips and haws which, though they had no leaves of their own, would tuck in among the laurels and yew that they could gather from their garden. They gathered sprays of spruce and fir, still fragrant even at this time of the year, and Vicky picked up a dozen or more cones that she intended painting either silver or gold to add a splash more colour to the sombre background of dark leaves.

Suddenly there was a shout from Fergus. For a moment she could not see him. Then he called again and she looked up. He was sitting astride the bough of a big tree, and in his hand was a mass of pale green foliage.

"Mistletoe!" he announced triumphantly. "Catch!"

And then, as he scrambled down: "That'll please Maggie! She adores being kissed under the mistletoe, though she always boxes my ears and pretends she doesn't!"

They laughed together, and Vicky's heart sang. She had no illusions. Fergus was going to marry Sybil, but none the less she knew that she was sharing something with him now that she did not think Sybil ever would. Of course, it was true that only a little while ago she would never have thought it possible for Fergus to unbend like this, so perhaps she was wrong about Sybil as well. And yet she did not think so. Surely it was easier to read another woman's character than a man's, and about Sybil she could not help feeling that there was something — calculating.

She dismissed the thought immediately. It was an unpleasant word, and out of keeping on a day like this. But her face must have grown suddenly serious, for Fergus noticed it. But he misunderstood its signifi-

141

cance. For he laid his hand on her shoulder and said gently:

"Vicky, sometimes the gods let one have a golden day that lives for ever. This is one of them. Don't tarnish it by looking back — or forward. Live just for the moment."

It was so unlike him that she could not disguise her surprise, and Fergus laughed ruefully.

"I know. It doesn't sound like me! Perhaps it isn't really. But don't you know that even a sobersides like me occasionally feels the need of relaxation? And that it only does harm if one is not willing to take up responsibilities again once it is over."

She smiled, well content. He was sharing his golden day with her, and it would certainly live for ever in her heart. There would be a poignant ache, too, because its beauty had been so transient, but she would not think of that now. She would do as he said, live for the moment.

And there was nothing to mar their day. After they had stowed all their booty away in the wagon, Fergus got out Maggie's basket and, sitting in the winter sun, they shared its contents, right down to the imperial mints that Maggie had tucked into a corner.

By the time they got home it was dark, but there was a welcome fire in the hall that brought a sense of well-being after the freshness of the December air.

They had tea with Mrs. Imray, sitting in front of the fire and toasting crumpets as they wanted them — the only way, according to Fergus. He seemed blissfully unaware that he ate the lion's share of the plateful and that Vicky was surreptitiously slipping some that were supposed to be hers on to his plate. She poured out innumerable cups of tea for him as well.

For a long time they sat on in a room lit only by the firelight and the one small light by Mrs. Imray's day bed. Then the two women realised that they were doing all the talking and that Fergus was silent — for a very good reason. He was fast asleep.

For a while Vicky sat still, content to watch the

strong face that was somehow vulnerable in the unconsciousness of sleep. Then she got quietly up, intending to go to her room to change for the evening. But as she passed Mrs. Imray, the older woman put out her hand and Vicky held the thin, twisted fingers in her own warm ones. Then gently she released them and went upstairs.

She hesitated for a moment in choosing her dress, and finally chose one that she had never worn at Hawthornden. It was an informal dinner dress of fine soft wool, the colour of burgundy. It had no trimming of any sort, so round her neck she fastened the snake-like links of a heavy gold necklace that had been her grandmother's. For a moment she looked gravely at her reflection; then she went slowly downstairs.

And at the bottom of them stood Fergus. His hair was rumpled and there was still the shadow of sleep in his eyes, but as he saw Vicky it cleared away and he regarded her very intently. He made no comment, but Vicky knew from his expression that he was admiring her appearance, and she smiled confidently up at him.

"Mother tells me that I must apologise to you for going off to sleep like that," he announced. "Will you forgive me?"

"Of course," Vicky said rather breathlessly.

They stood in silence for a moment as if neither quite knew what to say, and then Fergus said abruptly:

"I must go and change. Will you keep Mother company for a little while?"

Later they had dinner alone together, and though they found little to talk about, there was no feeling of strain, for the sense of well-being that the day had brought was still with them and their thoughts were of what they had shared.

After dinner, at his mother's request, Fergus went to the piano and played. It came as a surprise to Vicky to realise that he was a musician of no small merit and as, softly and unobtrusively, he wandered from Bach to Handel and back again to Bach she found herself wondering if there were still more facets to the character of this man whom she had both disliked and despised. And then, suddenly, he said:

"Come and sing, Vicky!" and before she could protest, she found herself standing by his elbow singing to his accompaniment as if it were the most natural thing in the world. Her voice had never been trained, but she trilled away happily when he started playing "Cherry Ripe" and "Comin' Through The Rye".

There was gentle applause from Mrs. Imray and Maggie, who had come in to listen. Encouraged by that, Vicky suggested "Sally in Our Alley" and Maggie put in a plea for "Annie Laurie".

Then, firmly, Fergus shut down the lid.

"That's all for tonight," he insisted. His eyes met Maggie's and she nodded ever so slightly. Unexciting though the entertainment had been, it was quite enough for Mrs. Imray. She was lying back on her pillows, and though her smile was as gay and tender as ever, her face was rather white. Vicky, following his glance, understood his anxiety and contrived a little yawn which suggested that it was for her benefit that Fergus had put a stop to her performance.

But something prompted her to bend over Mrs. Imray as she said good night and, against her usual custom, to kiss her. Mrs. Imray responded affectionately and before Vicky stood erect she heard the older woman whisper:

"I have not had such a happy evening for many, many years! Thank you, Vicky!"

And Fergus, escorting her to the foot of the stairs, added his thanks. He said, softly:

"Bless you, Vicky, for all you've done for my mother!" and, as he had done once before, lifted her hand to his lips.

And Vicky went up to bed with her heart singing and the hand that he had kissed held against her cheek.

The next morning when she ran downstairs, she

found Fergus standing in almost the same place as she had left him last night. But there was such a change in his appearance that her heart missed a beat. The face he lifted as he heard her approach was strained and white and there was a perceptible droop of his shoulders — involuntarily Vicky glanced to the door of his mother's room, and Fergus's eyes followed hers.

"No, Vicky, there is nothing for you to do — now!" he said heavily, and Vicky understood.

CHAPTER TEN

THE FIRST few days after Mrs. Imray's death were very busy ones, particularly for Vicky. It had come as a great blow to Maggie to lose her old friend, and she was thankful to let Vicky take the management of the house more or less into her own hands. Nor did Fergus find fault with the arrangement. In fact, he, like Maggie, was grateful to her. He was not the type of man to make a parade of his grief, but the tie between him and his mother had been a very strong one. Moreover, there were many duties that inevitably fell to him, including writing personal letters to various relatives.

Inevitably, since most of them lived at a distance, there was the necessity of putting some of them up for a day or so, and Vicky took over the task of making these arrangements.

Among the letters Fergus wrote was one to Sybil, and she, when she read it, experienced rather more strongly than any sense of regret, one of annoyance that Fergus had not telephoned or wired to her. In such circumstances she felt that her place was by his side, and she saw clearly enough that, in her absence, the duties which she felt should have been indisputably hers would fall to Vicky.

Not that, for a moment, she thought Vicky was at all interested in Fergus, but she felt a growing necessity for establishing herself in Fergus's life, and this situation would have given her just the opportunity. However, it was still not too late to do something about it. She terminated her holiday abruptly and returned, first of all to Lenster to pick up suitable clothes, and then, without stopping to get in touch with Fergus, straight down to Hawthornden.

Vicky opened the door to her. A Vicky with black smudges under her eyes and a serious face.

"Vicky, my dear little girl!" Sybil said, genuinely

startled at the girl's appearance. "This has all been too much for you!"

"It's all right," Vicky said, her heart sinking uncontrollably. It had been rather wonderful to know that Fergus was relying on her, that she could relieve him of some of his burden and see that he was properly cared for. But now, of course, he would turn to Sybil and she must take a back seat. "Won't you come in? Mr. Imray is out at the moment, but we are expecting him back at any time."

"We?" Sybil asked sharply.

"Maggie and I," Vicky explained. "Would you like some tea?"

"I should," Sybil replied gratefully. "But don't you worry about it. I can see to it myself. I know where everything is."

"It isn't any trouble —" Vicky said, but Sybil put her arm round the younger girl's shoulders and smiled at her.

"I think you've done about enough already," she said gently. "And you don't have to treat me as a guest, you know! Besides, I should like to have a word with Maggie."

She turned and walked down the hall, and Vicky watched her go without a word. What was there that she could either say or do when everything that Sybil had said was perfectly true and entirely natural? She stood there for a moment, undecided what to do, and then went quietly up to her own room so that, when Fergus came in, it was Sybil who greeted him.

"I had to come, Fergus!" she said, taking both his hands in hers. "You should have sent for me!"

"My dear, and curtail your well-earned holiday to an even greater degree?" he replied. "No, that would have been most unfair to you. Besides, we've managed. Vicky has been a perfect trump. Where is she, by the way?"

"Up in her room," Sybil said, hiding her irritation with difficulty. "I think the poor child was thankful to be relieved of any more duties now that I have come."

147

"Did she say so?" Fergus asked sharply.

"No," Sybil knew the value of truth as well as anyone. "But — it is pretty obvious that she is desperately tired and overstrained. She seemed very glad to have the opportunity for a rest when I suggested it."

Fergus was silent. His fair brows were knitted in a heavy frown, and he stared unseeingly into the fire by which they were standing.

"I suppose I've put too much of a burden on her," he admitted at length. "But she has been so willing, and I —"

"Have needed someone on whom to rely," Sybil finished gently. "I know. That is why I say I wish you had sent for me at once. Surely you knew I would have come, Fergus?"

Maggie came in at that moment, so Fergus made no reply, but Sybil was not dissatisfied with her efforts.

"There's a meal ready for you," Maggie said rather shortly. She never had liked Sybil and she made no bones about it. If Master Fergus wanted to marry her that was his business, but so far as Maggie was concerned, that would mean she left Hawthornden. She had all too clear a knowledge of what the house would be like with Sybil as its mistress — and nothing that had happened that day had altered her opinion.

"Thanks," Fergus said indifferently. "I'll come in a minute or two."

"Oh, Fergus, no, you mustn't neglect yourself," Sybil said quickly. "Please come and have your food now while it is nice and hot."

"Miss Vicky worked real hard to get everything nice for you," Maggie commented as she brushed up the hearth. "She went down to the village and fair bullied the butcher into finding a nice steak for you!"

"Did she, though!" Fergus smiled. He turned to Sybil. "Huggins is about six foot six and broad in proportion. I'd like to have seen Vicky tackling him! I'll come at once, Maggie."

"Fine," Maggie commented laconically, perfectly well aware that she had put a spoke in Sybil's wheel and rejoicing thereat.

But Sybil was no fool. She could read Maggie's mind with ease and knew that she had got an enemy there, but it did not worry her very much. In spite of Fergus's affection for the old woman he was not a man who would allow anyone to dictate to him, and the more Maggie tried to do so, the less notice Fergus would take of her.

All the same, Sybil was very careful to do nothing to which Fergus himself could take exception, contenting herself with a place well in the background while other relatives were present. It was not until the house was empty of visitors that she made a decided move.

Vicky, with no wish to be a third at what would otherwise be a *tête-à-tête* announced that she intended having her meal with Maggie in order to keep her company. Fergus said gently:

"That's sweet of you, Vicky!" and made no objection, as Vicky had known he would not.

When she had left them, Sybil turned to Fergus.

"That child has improved tremendously, Fergus!"

"I think she has," he agreed.

"Well, as you know, I thought you were taking on too big a job, but I was wrong," Sybil said generously. "It has done her all the good in the world to be here. One wonders, perhaps, whether the cure is permanent or not. Of course, she hasn't been here very long, really. I could wish for her sake that it could be longer."

"Could be —" he began. "I don't understand, Sybil."

Sybil spread her hands deprecatingly.

"Well, Fergus, she can hardly stay on here now, can she?"

"Not to look after my mother, of course," Fergus agreed. "But I can find her other work —"

"I don't think you quite understand," Sybil said gently. "I know that in your eyes, Vicky is little more than a child, but I am afraid that would not stop the possibility of gossip."

"Gossip?" It was clearly a new idea to him. "Oh,

nonsense, Sybil! She is, as you say, little more than a child and, besides, there is Maggie."

"I know. But surely you know, Fergus, that a servant, however respectable and otherwise suitable, is not regarded as an adequate chaperon in such circumstances. I suppose the idea is that as an employee she is under your orders or might shut her eyes to any irregularities rather than lose her job."

Fergus was silent, and Sybil wondered whether she had gone too far, but his next remark reassured her.

"Thanks, Sybil, for calling my attention to it. I must say it had not occurred to me, but I can see that it is a point of view."

"I'm afraid it is," Sybil said regretfully. "And it would be unfair to Vicky to ignore it. What a pity there is no idea of her marrying that nice Pickard boy!"

Fergus pushed back his chair rather abruptly.

"As far as I know, there is every possibility of her marrying him. In fact, more now than before."

"More — I don't understand," Sybil looked puzzled.

"I imagine that money has been the main obstacle," Fergus explained briefly. "Pickard will be all right eventually, but in the meantime, he is pretty short. However, Vicky will not come to him exactly penniless."

"But I thought you said there weren't two ha' pennies to rub together!" Sybil reminded him.

"Nor are there — as far as her father's estate is concerned," Fergus agreed. "But my mother has provided for Vicky for some time to come."

"Your mother —!" Sybil was too startled to hide her surprise.

"Yes. Mother has created a Trust which will provide Vicky with an income of two hundred and fifty pounds a year for the next five years. That should see them over comfortably," Fergus explained.

"But —" gasped Sybil. "Two hundred and fifty pounds a year! Why, that means a capital of — of something over twelve thousand pounds is locked up for five years!"

"About that," Fergus agreed curtly.

"But surely, that is unfair to you!" Sybil protested, too startled to be discreet. "I mean, your mother knew Vicky for such a short time, and you had every right to expect —"

"My mother had perfect freedom to conduct her affairs as she wished, and I have no quarrel to pick with the way in which she did so," Fergus told her. "And, at least, it will relieve your mind of any anxiety for Vicky. She will, I imagine, be getting married fairly soon. Until then, I intend that she shall stay on here, and if that is going to cause gossip, then I will live in Lenster in an hotel. But whatever happens, Vicky is not going to be turned out of what is, after all, her only home. And that I intend to make absolutely clear to everybody who is at all interested."

"Yes, of course," Sybil said mechanically. And then, collecting her wits: "Vicky is a very lucky girl to have found two such friends as your mother and you, Fergus. I hope that she is grateful!"

Her tone suggested that she had doubts about that, but Fergus did not make any comment. And when he spoke again, it was to introduce quite a different and entirely uncontroversial subject.

Actually, when Vicky first heard of the bequest, she was much too surprised to experience any other emotion.

"But I don't understand," she told Fergus. "Why should your mother have done this? She had only known me for such a short time —"

"Long enough to have grown very fond of you, Vicky," Fergus assured her. "And I imagine it gave her very great pleasure to know that she had made some sort of provision for your future."

Vicky looked up at him with troubled eyes.

"Do you want me to have it?" she asked.

"Certainly," he said promptly. "In fact, I regard it as a matter of honour to see that my mother's wishes are carried out. I do hope that you will not be difficult about this, Vicky."

She hesitated still, but at length she said:

"No, I am not going to be difficult. There is not so much kindness about that one can afford to refuse any, and this is the kindest thing that anyone has ever done for me. I — I shan't waste it."

"Good girl," Fergus said rather absently. "And — you will stay on here — at least for a while?"

"Well —" she began doubtfully, and for a moment he thought that she was going to make the same objection that Sybil had to such a plan. "If there is any work that I can do. I couldn't just do nothing."

"I wouldn't ask you to," Fergus said coolly. "Perhaps your duties will not be clearly defined, but they will be none the less real. For one thing, I want you to relieve Maggie of the management of the house. She has earned a rest, and I don't think you will find her difficult. Then there is Larry to exercise, and —"

He stopped because Vicky was smiling gravely at him and shaking her head.

"I think you are just trying to make things easy for me," she said reproachfully.

"Not at all," denied Fergus firmly. "I told you that it would not be so easy to define your duties, but that will probably make them all the more demanding. I understand that most women who run a house insist that their work is never done. You will probably find the same thing."

Vicky did not reply, and Fergus went on:

"Perhaps I had better make the situation a little clearer. The worst of the winter is yet to come, and I have decided to take a room at the Royal in Lenster for a time. It is too much to expect Maggie to keep everything going, and I shall be very much obliged if you will stay. In the spring, possibly we can make a different arrangement —"

Then she understood. It was natural enough that, now he had not got his mother to consider, he should think of his own comfort first, but somehow that argument did not convince her. What was far more likely was that he felt free now to think of his own happiness, and to live in Lenster would give him the opportunity of seeing far more of Sybil than he had been able to do in the past. He might even have felt that his other ties had meant that Sybil had not really had a fair deal. Three months' courtship and then marriage — was that his idea?

"Well?" he asked.

"I could not take it on if you did not come down sometimes to see that everything was all right," she said slowly.

"Of course I shall come," he answered promptly. "Does that mean you will carry on?"

"Yes," she promised. "In the meantime, anyhow."

He gave a sigh of relief, but whether because had agreed or because she had made it clear that she understood it was only a temporary arrangement, she did not know.

The house seemed very quiet when Fergus had left it. But Vicky found plenty to do. At Maggie's suggestion they turned the two rooms which Mrs. Imray had used back to their original use. One had, so Maggie told her, been used as a little breakfast-room and the other had been Mrs. Imray's own sitting-room. At first Vicky had felt reluctant to make the changes, feeling, somehow, that it implied a disloyalty to the memory of Mrs. Imray, but Maggie had taken a common-sense stand.

"These things have to be done sooner or later. It is better to do them at once — better for Master Fergus, too. He's young and his life is before him, it isn't right for him to look back all the time."

And after that, Vicky made no further objections. But when, in the big, formal drawing-room which had been carefully sheeted ever since she had been in the house, she had come across a painting of Mrs. Imray as a younger woman, she had the odd-job man in to lift it down and hang it in the sitting-room. She did it without consulting Maggie, but the old woman's approval was instant.

"That'll please Master Fergus," she said cordially. "You're a thoughtful lassie, Miss Vicky. And it comes from the heart, not the head, like some I could name!"

Vicky said nothing. She had realised long ago that there was no love lost between Sybil and Maggie, but she did not feel that anything she said would improve matters. In fact, it might only serve to make things worse. And though, now, she could not help agreeing with Maggie, she knew quite well that the situation was not entirely Sybil's fault. Maggie was not an easy person to get on with unless one had the luck to get on her soft side.

It was a fortnight before Fergus came down, and then it was only for a night.

Both Vicky and Maggie were disappointed at that, but while Vicky kept her feelings to herself, Maggie was very frank.

"Miss Vicky has worked her fingers to the bone," she insisted. "The least you could do is to stay awhile to show your appreciation — and take her out for a bit of entertainment!"

"Maggie!" Vicky protested.

"It's true," Maggie retorted calmly. "The child hasn't put her nose out of doors except to go riding or messages down to the village. Young people need to go dancing and seeing plays and such-like. You ought to see that she does, Master Fergus!"

"Yes, of course," he said slowly. "But hasn't —" and stopped abruptly. He turned to Vicky. "Maggie is quite right, of course. But you know that you are entitled to time off. Haven't you been taking it?"

She felt a deep reluctance to discuss Gil with him, for now that she knew Gil's secret it would be so difficult to keep Fergus from guessing the situation — and it wasn't fair play to let that happen.

"It's just that we have been extra busy for a little while," she explained carefully. "It will be all right now."

"I see. Well, make sure that it is. I can't have Maggie bullying me like this. It makes me feel the worst sort of criminal!"

Vicky smiled and then, to her relief, the subject dropped. But, unknown to her, Maggie took it up again with Fergus.

"That laddie hasn't been near the place since the night of the Hospital Ball," she told him. "Nor written nor telephoned."

Fergus looked up sharply.

"Has she seemed unhappy?" he asked.

"She's not one to wear her heart on her sleeve, any more than you yourself," Maggie answered. "But — I caught her in tears one day. She didn't know I saw, and I said nothing. She's aye listening for the telephone, too."

"I see," Fergus scowled.

"There's many a heart been caught on the rebound," Maggie remarked after a brief silence.

"No doubt," Fergus did not sound particularly interested. "Well — I must be going. However, I'll be down at the week-end."

"Will Miss Sybil be coming?" Maggie asked casually.

"I'm not sure. I'll let you know. Now I must see Vicky for a moment. Vicky!" he called, and when she came: "Look, there's a big packet of correspondence I'm expecting to come here by post. From London. If it comes, do you think you could bring it in to the office for me?"

"Of course," she promised.

"Right! Give me a ring before you start. I want to be there to take it from you. It's rather important."

"Very well. I'll remember," Vicky said, and a few moments later, Fergus left.

It was a trifling thing to promise, and if Vicky gave it a second thought, it was simply to be glad that she could be of use to Fergus. But actually, the packet did not arrive until the second post on Friday afternoon, and, balancing it on one hand, Vicky discussed Fergus's orders doubtfully.

"I know he said it was urgent, but after all, he will be down this evening. I shall hardly be able to get into Lenster before it is time to come home again."

"Nor you will," Maggie agreed gravely. "But Master Fergus knows what he's talking about. Maybe it's to do with some office business."

"Then it seems strange that they should be sent here," Vicky suggested. "Oh, well, I'd better ring Mr. Imray up and see what he says."

And Fergus was quite definite. He certainly had meant what he said. She would just have time to catch the four o'clock train and she was to take a taxi to the office. He wanted the packet as quickly as possible.

"My goodness, he's in a hurry," Maggie commented when Vicky, scrambling into her outdoor clothes, told her what had happened.

Vicky was shown immediately into Fergus's office, and he held out his hand for the packet she carried.

"Thank you, Vicky, for being so prompt," he said and motioned her to a chair. He tore open the envelope and became completely immersed in its contents. He scribbled a few notes and appeared to make a calculation and then he rang for his secretary.

"Oh, Miss Tanner, send off the letter to Price and Venway, will you? They've sent me the necessary certificates now."

"Yes, Mr. Imray," Miss Tanner said meekly. She was too well trained a secretary to glance at Vicky in any obvious way, but Vicky knew quite well that there was little in her appearance that the other woman had not contrived to absorb, and her feet fidgeted restlessly.

"Can I go now, Mr. Imray?" she asked, and Fergus looked up as if he had forgotten she was there.

"Oh — I'll drive you back, Vicky," he said casually. "I'll be ready in about a quarter of an hour."

"But I've got a return ticket," Vicky objected.

"Have you? Never mind, you can use that up some other time. I'll ring through to Maggie and let her know you'll be a bit later." And before she could protest, he had lifted his telephone.

Vicky sank back in her chair. It did seem rather silly not to go back in the comfort of Fergus's car when he was using it, anyhow, but suddenly she became frightened. In the car they would be in a little world of their own, cut off from other people. It would be almost impossible to maintain that friendly, impersonal ..tude that was difficult at the best of times. And so when Fergus said casually:

"I want to have a meal before we start. I didn't have time for any lunch," she made no protest. It was putting off the drive home even if only for a little while.

He took her to a restaurant that, in the old days, she had often gone to herself, but as it happened there were none of her old friends present. And Vicky, starved of the bright lights that had once been so familiar, was young enough to forget everything else and simply enjoy herself.

At first Fergus appeared content simply to eat and indulge in desultory conversation but after a while, he, too, seemed to regain his spirits, and Vicky found the courage to say:

"You looked awfully worried when I came into the office. Was anything the matter?"

"Not — really. It was just that I had had rather a disagreeable interview during the afternoon, and I suppose I hadn't got rid of the effects of it. Thank you for noticing, Vicky!"

It was obvious that he had completely got over his depression now and was enjoying himself sufficiently well not to want to hurry over the meal. Indeed, when a little later the dance band began to play, he appeared to take it for granted that they should dance. And Vicky, remembering what he had said about snatching golden hours as they came, slipped into his arms and forgot everything except that they were together.

It was during the third dance that Vicky suddenly saw Gil. He was dining at a table on the other side of the room with a fair-haired girl who was gazing adoringly up into his face, and as Vicky noticed them, they, too, got up and danced. It was very obvious that the two of them were on very good terms, and Vicky gave a little sigh of relief. It might not be very flattering that Gil could so soon be happy with another girl, but she found it infinitely reassuring. She would have hated to know that because of her Gil was never to find happiness.

And then, suddenly, Fergus saw Gil. Vicky knew that he had because she felt him start and then he glanced down at her.

"Yes, I've seen them," she murmured, and was going to make some comment about the coincidence of seeing them here when she realised that Fergus was steering her back to their table.

"Would you like to go?" he asked, and Vicky looked at him in surprise. Surely he did not imagine that she was in love with Gil — that it had distressed her to see him with another girl? But he did! There was no misunderstanding the sympathy in his eyes. It should have been the simplest thing in the world for Vicky to have said: "No, why should I? It's the thing I hoped would happen!" But for some reason or other, it was not, and instead she found herself saying:

"Why not let us finish our dinner first?"

"You've plenty of courage, Vicky! All right, we'll finish then."

Even so, it was not more than another quarter of an hour before they left. Gil was far too absorbed in his partner to have noticed them, and Vicky was glad. It might have been embarrassing for him, poor darling, and he was having such a good time!

The garage where Fergus had left his car was only just round the corner, and in a few minutes they were on their way, Vicky well tucked in with a warm rug.

Fergus drove in silence. Vicky, watching his set face, wished that she had explained the situation to him as soon as he had seen Gil, but now it was too late. She did not feel that Fergus would believe her and after all, the only proof that she could offer was to say: "I can't be in love with Gil because I love you!" So she said nothing.

And it was Fergus who finally broke the silence. Without slackening the speed of the car or even glancing towards her he said abruptly:

"Vicky, will you marry me?"

CHAPTER ELEVEN

FOR A moment Vicky was too amazed to reply. Then she said rather breathlessly:

"But — why?"

Unconsciously her hands clenched as she waited for his reply, but when it came, it did not really answer her question, for Fergus simply said, coolly:

"Why not?"

Vicky found herself shaking her head.

"Oh, no! One has to have more of a reason for marrying than just that there is no reason why one shouldn't!"

"Does one?" Fergus asked dryly. "Judging by a good many of the marriages I see, that appears to be regarded as a perfectly good reason! However, in our case — we are both rather lonely people, Vicky, and I think we could at least give one another the comfort of companionship. That is quite a lot, you know."

"Yes," Vicky whispered. The comfort of companionship. It was indeed a great deal. But was it enough? "Only — if there is someone else that — that one of the people loves — even if, for some reason, nothing will come of it — is it quite — quite —"

She floundered for the word she wanted to express her right meaning and Fergus, thinking he understood what was in her mind, said quietly:

"I don't think anything is so likely to wipe out the past, Vicky, as looking towards the future. You and I can do that. And — second thoughts are sometimes best."

Vicky, dazed at the suddenness of it all, could only conclude that something had gone wrong between him and Sybil, though what it could be, she could not imagine. But it was not possible to shut her heart to the fear that, perhaps, some time in the future, if she were to marry Fergus, he and Sybil would find that, after all, there had been only some misunderstanding that could have been cleared up between them. Fergus, tied to herself when he wanted to be free to marry Sybil — that would be unthinkable —

And then, as she hesitated, Fergus's hand fell warm and sustaining over hers.

"Trust me, Vicky," he said quietly. "It will be all right!"

And Vicky, blind now to everything but the knowledge that she could, if she had the courage, be his wife, heard a voice that she hardly recognised as her own whisper: "Very well!"

For a moment longer Fergus's hand lay on hers. Then he said: "Thank you, Vicky!" very gently and took his hand away.

They drove in silence for a while. What Fergus was thinking of Vicky had no idea, but her own thoughts were in a whirl. She was going to marry Fergus. Not because he loved her but because he was lonely and unhappy — she vowed in her heart that she would give him the comfort he needed, asking little for herself but the satisfaction of knowing that he had turned to her. And perhaps in the future, he would find his heart so warmed that he would be able to love her a little —

She started as his voice cut across her thoughts.

"Vicky — can you be ready to marry me early in the New Year? By the end of January at the latest?"

"Why — yes, Fergus, if you want me to," she said promptly.

"I do," he insisted. "And — shall we tell Maggie tonight? I should like her to know before we make it public."

"Yes, of course," she said hurriedly. "But — could it be tomorrow that we tell her? I — I want to get used to the idea myself first!"

She heard him laugh softly at that, and, after a moment's hesitation, laughed as well.

"I think telling it to someone else is probably the one thing that will make it seem real to you, Vicky," he suggested. "In any case, I rather fancy Maggie will guess!"

"Oh, why?" she asked quickly. "I mean, it isn't as if —" and checked herself shortly.

"As if there is much to see?" he asked, probably quite unconscious, Vicky thought, of the rather bitter note in his voice. "No, possibly not. All the same, Maggie has second sight where these things are concerned. You'll see!"

And, indeed, Maggie took one look at them and then stood waiting, her hands on her hips, her face agog with anticipation.

Fergus turned to Vicky.

"There, what did I tell you? I never have been able to keep a secret from Maggie! Tell her, Vicky!"

"Mr. Imray — Fergus and I are going to be married," Vicky said hurriedly, and Maggie beamed as she swept the girl into a warm embrace. Her first words were typical — and served to relieve the strain of the moment.

"It must have been sheer inspiration!" she announced. "I had Tebitt kill a fowl today for your dinner tomorrow — and there's your favourite pudding as well, Master Fergus!"

Fergus and Vicky caught each other's eyes — it was the first time their glances had crossed since Fergus had asked her to marry him — and they were unable to restrain their amusement. To Vicky it seemed as if a great load had been lifted from her shoulders. Surely it was a good augury that they could find humour in the same things —

"Oh, maybe it's funny. But there's nothing like a good meal for sustaining the emotions!" Maggie declared, and then, with sudden wistfulness: "Will you be wanting me to stay on, Miss Vicky?"

"Oh, Maggie, of course!" Vicky said impulsively. "It wouldn't be like home without you here!"

The old woman went off, well pleased, to the kitchen, and Fergus, as he helped Vicky off with her coat, slipped an arm round her shoulders.

"You couldn't have said anything that would please Maggie better than that!" he said softly. "Thank you, Vicky!" and lightly brushed her cheek with his lips.

Vicky's dark lashes flickered on her cheeks. It was far from being a lover's kiss, but it was the first one she had ever had from Fergus, and it sent her blood racing.

"I'm afraid I didn't stop to think what I was saying," she admitted. "I just took it for granted that it was what you wanted as well —"

His arm tightened for a second round her shoulders.

"You can take it for granted, Vicky, that what comes from the heart, as that did, can never be wrong, least of all in my eyes!"

Then he let her go.

The formal announcement of their engagement appeared in both *The Times* and the local paper on the same day. Vicky had almost decided to ring Gil up and tell him herself, but the thought of the blonde girl had deterred her. She did not want to do anything which might make Gil feel she regarded him as in any way her property. None the less, she was pleased and touched when Gil rang her up and wished her every happiness.

"It's rather sudden, though, isn't it?" he asked a little anxiously.

"Yes, perhaps it is," Vicky admitted, wishing that he had not said that. "But, after all, there is no reason why we shouldn't get married immediately."

"No," Gil admitted. "Imray is one of those lucky beggars who has a good job, a house and a handsome income. There's nothing to stop him. Except —" he paused as if he did not quite know how to put his thought into words.

"Except?" Vicky said rather more sharply than she intended.

"You're quite sure your Rochester has no skeletons in the cupboard?" Gil said slowly and, troubled, Vicky realised that he was trying to half-conceal a very real anxiety under the jesting words.

"No!" she said vigorously. "No skeletons! If it

interests you, I was up in the attics just yesterday!"

"And no mad wives?" he asked flippantly.

"No, nor anything else!" she averred.

There was a little pause.

"Well, once again, Vicky, every happiness! Cheers!" And he had gone.

Vicky hung up with a sense of loss. Gil had really gone out of her life when she had to tell him she did not love him, but this, somehow, seemed much more final. She remembered her wish, at which he had laughed, however ruefully, that he were her brother, and found herself wishing it again.

Something kept her from telling Fergus of the call, not because she was afraid to in one sense, but because Gil belonged to the past — the past from which she and Fergus were resolutely turning their faces — and she did not want to do anything to remind him of it.

Whether he heard from Sybil she did not know, but she thought that it was unlikely. Instinct told her that they had parted in anger, and so it was she who would probably ring him up in order to wish him happiness. But actually, Vicky did not give the matter much thought. She was very busy, for Fergus had insisted that she should make any alterations in the house that she saw fit, and although in the main she was satisfied with things as they were, many of the rooms had not been used for some time and needed a thorough overhaul to make them really liveable.

Fergus's own bedroom she left exactly as it was, thinking that the familiarity of it would always be a refuge to him but, after considerable thought and very evidently with Maggie's approval, she re-arranged the principal bedroom, putting in lighter, younger-looking furniture and buying new curtain material. The dressing-room which opened off it, she left as it was except that she bought a couple of very beautiful modern pictures, one of a rough sea and the other of a tranquil inland pool. They were the perfect complement of one another and caught the eye as soon as one entered the room. Fergus made no comment on the arrangements she had made, but he seemed well content and he approved of her pictures unreservedly.

And then, unexpectedly, he had to go away. He came to breakfast one morning with an open letter in his hand and a rueful expression on his face.

"A client of mine who has been dying for years has decided she wants her will altered again. And being convinced, as she always is, that her end is imminent, insists on my coming to her at once! She's been staying with some of her family in Manchester over Christmas, and I expect that is what is at the bottom of it. She's a quarrelsome old thing, and she probably wants to disinherit somebody and benefit someone else. I'll have to go, Vicky, and I can't see myself getting away in less than three or four days. She likes to feel that she can still give orders and, poor old thing, it's about the only pleasure she has!"

Vicky laughed.

"Is she very rich?" she asked idly.

"Rich enough to be a very good client," he admitted. "But it isn't only that. We have looked after her family's affairs for several generations, and there is a certain amount of responsibility, one feels. I may be able to keep her from doing anything very silly." He folded the letter up and put it into his pocket. "You don't mind, Vicky? You'll be all right?"

"Of course I shall!" she said reassuringly. "I've got quite a lot to do — I must see about a wedding dress, for one thing."

"Yes, of course," he agreed, and she saw a shadow fall across his face. "Vicky, there is just one thing — do you mind not going to Sybil for it? I know she's one of the leading fashion experts here, but all the same —"

It was the first time that Sybil's name had been mentioned between them, and Vicky felt as if a cold hand had clutched at her heart.

"Actually, it hadn't occurred to me to think of going to her," she said as naturally as she could. "You see, I never did, in the old days. I thought of going to the places I used to —"

"Yes, that's the idea," he agreed, and turned to his breakfast with an expression of some relief on his face.

When he had gone, Vicky was conscious of a feeling of depression. Was it possible, she wondered, really to put the past behind one or was it always going to crop up like this? Then, resolutely, she refused to think about it any more and got on with the day's tasks. And in spite of Maggie's remonstrances, she worked until late in the evening.

"The minute Master Fergus takes his eyes off you!" Maggie lamented. "You'll be tired out! You're like a ghost now!"

"A ghost with a dirty face!" Vicky said lightly, as she caught sight of her reflection in the mirror. "Never mind, Maggie, it is only for once, and it means I shall be free to go into Lenster tomorrow and buy my wedding dress!"

"Aye, you should be getting that," Maggie agreed, cheering up.

And, early in the morning, Vicky started off. In spite of everything, her heart beat more quickly as she made her request. They both felt that a very quiet wedding was desirable, but all the same, Fergus had evidently taken it for granted that she would wear white. And if the assistant who attended her thought that she was rather grave for such an occasion, she made no comment. She remembered Vicky, having frequently served her in the past, and she had heard of the engagement — she could hardly have failed to do so, for plenty of her other clients had had something to say about it — most of them frankly considering Vicky both lucky and wise.

She had heard Fergus described as rather a dull person but having quite a lot of money, and that was quite enough to ensure good service for Vicky.

Vicky came out of the shop to find that it was practically lunch-time, and for a moment she hesitated. She must have a meal, but she felt disinclined to go to any of her old haunts, knowing that, if she were to meet any of her old friends, this time they

165

would seek her company all right. In a sense it did not matter. She was independent of their friendship now, but all the same, that sort of thing hurt and she did not want there to be a shadow cast over her happiness today.

So, after walking about rather aimlessly for a time, she went into a small restaurant to which she had never been before, and which seemed to be patronised largely by women of reasonably comfortable means. Probably those who had good jobs in the surrounding offices and shops. And that proved to be the case. She had hardly sat down before she heard someone speak to her by name and, turning round, she saw that it was Sybil.

The last person that she had wanted to meet; but obviously manners demanded that she should ask Sybil to share her table, and, after a moment's hesitation, Sybil sat down.

They talked of commonplace matters for a time and then, after their orders had been taken by the smart little waitress, Sybil said thoughtfully:

"I suppose you've come up to shop?"

"Yes," Vicky said briefly, and knew that her very brevity had told Sybil more than she had intended to. The older girl flinched.

"Your trousseau?" she asked, as if it caused her almost physical pain to say the words.

Vicky nodded. After all, a wedding dress was, she supposed, part of one's trousseau, so there was no need to say more. She waited for Sybil to make some comment, but the silence continued between them until it lay heavy and oppressive like a cloud pregnant with storm.

And then Sybil broke the silence. For a moment the muscles at the corners of her mouth worked uncontrollably and then, desperately but almost in a whisper, as if she were speaking to herself she said:

"If only I knew what to do! If only I knew!"

Very erect, Vicky faced her. Sybil's words had cast a sudden chill over her. But she did not pretend to herself that she was ignorant of what they meant. Sybil, as well as Fergus, knew the reason for his unexpected proposal to herself and that it must have been a quarrel of some sort. Otherwise, surely, since Sybil had been so much one of the family, she would have continued to be. So now she said quietly:

"You had better do what you feel to be the right thing — no matter if you do hurt people's feelings."

Yet still Sybil hesitated. More than once she had deliberated on the advisability of getting into touch with Vicky and making her last bid to marry Fergus, but always she had hesitated. She could tell a convincing tale, she knew, but she, unlike everybody else, apparently, had always seen the probability that Vicky would fall in love with Fergus. Consequently, whatever story she told, Vicky would be unlikely to take any notice of it simply because it did not suit her to. Besides, if she had written Vicky could have taken the letter to Fergus and would have listened eagerly, no doubt, to his denials, while a telephone conversation was somehow too casual to convey the seriousness of the situation. It was only now that, unexpectedly face to face with Vicky, she could not help making use of her undoubted histrionic powers.

She drew in a sharp breath as if she were going to speak, hesitated, and then took the plunge.

"I am the last person, Vicky, who ought to tell you this," she began very quietly. "Because I do not see how you can possibly believe that I am in the least disinterested. And yet — I am. You know, I'm not the sort of woman who makes many woman friends, but — I've always had a soft spot for you. You've had a rough time and you've shown plenty of courage. I admire that. My own life hasn't been so smooth that I can't appreciate what it means."

Vicky said nothing, because the only thing she wanted to do was to scream at Sybil to get on with her story, whatever it was. And perhaps Sybil realised it, for she went on, her eyes downcast, her forefinger tracing a pattern on the white cloth:

"There is no way of saying this tactfully, I'm afraid, Vicky. You see, Fergus and I were engaged.

Then, after Mrs. Imray's death he came to see me one evening and he deliberately picked a quarrel with me. It was so strange that I did not know what to do about it. I thought perhaps it simply meant that Fergus was over-wrought with what had happened, and in a day or so he would come to me and explain — but the only explanation I had was the news of his engagement to you." She paused, and, seeing that Vicky's hands were clenched at the edge of the table, she went on, well content with the effect that she was producing.

"If he had discovered that he did not love me," she went on in a low voice, "and that he did love you, there would have been nothing wrong about it. I should have had to accept the situation. One has to be practical about such things. The heart changes — that is all there is to be said about it. But as things are — Vicky, I don't expect you to believe me, but it is not only that I love Fergus far too well to let him do such a thing, but I like you far too much to allow him to do it to *you!* Please, please believe that!"

Did she believe it? Vicky hardly knew, but she heard herself saying through stiff lips:

"But why — if he loved you — there must have been a reason —"

"Yes," Sybil said sadly, "there was a reason. Don't you understand — even now?"

"No," Vicky said jerkily. "If you want me to know, you will have to tell me yourself."

"Mrs. Imray has left you some money, hasn't she?" Sybil said softly.

"Two hundred and fifty pounds a year for five years," Vicky acknowledged.

"Yes, well, I don't suppose that sounds a great deal even if you add it up. A total of twelve hundred and fifty pounds. Fergus could easily have paid you that amount and not felt it. But the way Mrs. Imray has done it means that for five years the capital that will be locked up in order to provide that income is — something over twelve thousand pounds!"

"No!" Vicky gasped. "It can't be!"

"By the time you take income tax into consideration — it certainly is," Sybil said coolly. "Now do you understand? Fergus is his mother's executor. He has everything under his thumb. None the less, you might think of engaging another solicitor to look after your interests. But if Fergus marries you, naturally you will leave things in his hands — and you will be perfectly free to take your two hundred and fifty a year without asking any awkward questions about capital. Now do you see?"

And Vicky was silent. Unbidden, memories returned to her mind. Fergus himself had told her that on the afternoon of the day that he had proposed to her, he had had a very unpleasant interview. It could only have been with Sybil. And when one came to think of it, how lame his arguments that they should get married had been! In the end, he had asked her to trust him blindly and she, listening to her heart and not her head, had done as she wished.

"You mustn't blame him too much," Sybil's voice seemed to come to her from a great distance. "It must have come as a great shock to him, and these days money is difficult to find, you know. I expect he had reckoned on what his mother would leave him — and I don't suppose he could afford to live nearly so comfortably with all that tied up. So many people are having to use capital nowadays, you know."

"Please!" Vicky begged urgently. "Please don't talk for a minute! I've got to think things out —"

"All right," Sybil agreed. "But there is just one thing I want to say, Vicky. If you love Fergus sincerely, don't let him do this! He's fine and decent really — I know that! But it must have been a sudden temptation —" She did not know whether Vicky heard her, but she knew quite well from her victim's agonised little face that there was no need to say anything more, and suddenly Vicky began to speak:

"I must go away!" she said hurriedly. "It is the only thing to do! I can't see Fergus again — I can't —"

Sybil was silent. This was exactly the reaction that

she had hoped for, but the most difficult part was now to come. She must help Vicky to go away — but she must not be too eager to offer help. So she waited, and her patience was rewarded.

"I shall telephone to Maggie and tell her that I am staying the night with friends. And I will write to Fergus breaking off our engagement," Vicky said in a small, tired voice. "I shall tell him that I have decided not to accept his mother's legacy — then he will not worry to come after me."

"Where will you go?" Sybil asked softly, and Vicky looked at her with haunted eyes.

"I don't know — somewhere right away. I shall have to get work —"

"Do you know of anyone who will give you a job — at once?" Sybil asked, and Vicky shook her head. "I wonder —" Sybil began, and hesitated. "Would you take on being a mannequin?"

"For you?" Vicky shrank back. "But I want to get out of Lenster!"

"No, not for me. For a friend of mine in London. Look, Vicky, I could, if you like, 'phone through to her at once and fix it up. I know she wants someone like you, because I had a letter from her just the other day. Don't let me over-persuade you but — there it is, if it is any good to you."

Vicky did not hesitate. To get away as far as possible from Lenster and Fergus was the only thing that mattered, and here was an opportunity ready to hand.

"Thank you, Sybil," she said tonelessly, and Sybil beckoned to the waitress.

"Our bill," she said briskly, and when the girl was about to argue added: "Yes, I know, we've hardly eaten anything, but my friend is not well —"

Outside in the street she turned and looked at Vicky.

"You'd better come back to my flat," she suggested. "I will telephone at once — and you can write your note to Fergus if you like!"

"Very well," Vicky agreed listlessly.

Sybil's luck held. She not only got through to London without any delay but she was able to get in touch with her friend. A few brief explanations and it was all fixed up. Vicky, listening to the disposal of herself and her affairs, felt oddly uninterested. After all, what mattered now? Fergus, the one person in all the world whom she had believed she could trust, was no better than anyone else. A self-seeker, putting money before everything —

"Vera is thrilled," Sybil said as she rang off. "She's got a winter show coming off next week. Of course, I told her that you were inexperienced, but she said that any girl who knows how to wear clothes will do. I'll write down her address and 'phone number. Actually, she lives at an hotel and she is engaging a room for you —"

"Thank you," Vicky said, taking the paper from her.

"And now, you had better write your letter —" Sybil suggested. She went to her bureau and took out some sheets, not of her headed paper but of similar, unheaded paper that she used if writing longer letters. An envelope, stamp. Sybil was very thorough. "I'll leave you alone," she said softly. "I don't suppose it will be easy —"

It was not. In fact, it was the most difficult letter Vicky had ever written, and at last she decided that the less said the better. For now, all that mattered was to make him understand that their engagement was broken. Afterwards, through a solicitor, she could inform him that she had decided not to accept his mother's bequest.

So, in her unformed, schoolgirl scrawl she wrote:

Dear Fergus,

I thought that we would be able to forget the past, but now I know we can't. It will always keep coming up between us, and so I've decided not to marry you. Please accept my decision. I know it will be best for us both if you do.

VICKY

And tucked it into an envelope. Sybil, when she came back into the room, saw it lying there and would have given her eyes to know what Vicky had said. But she ignored it, saying cheerfully:

"Now, I don't want to hustle you, but there is a train in half an hour! Would you like to catch it?"

"Yes," Vicky said briefly. "I'll telephone Maggie —"

Maggie proved to be rather difficult to satisfy. She wanted to know with whom Vicky was staying and if Fergus knew about it. Finally, in desperation, Vicky hung up.

Less than half an hour later, she was on her way to London. Sybil saw her off, and when the train vanished round the curve, drew what she felt was the first proper breath in hours. Heavens, it was incredible that in this day and age a girl could be so simple! Really, you could not blame cleverer people for taking advantage of it!

CHAPTER TWELVE

THERE was one thing that neither Vicky nor Sybil had taken into their calculations, and that was the degree of Maggie's anxiety.

It was reasonable enough, no doubt, to imagine that Vicky had met some old friend and had been persuaded to spend the night with her, but Maggie was not satisfied. The girl's voice had sounded unfamiliar and strained and, even more disturbing, she had ended the conversation so abruptly — cut off, in fact.

She hesitated for a while, but at last her anxiety got too much for her, and glancing at the clock she realised that her last chance of getting in touch with Fergus would be gone in a matter of ten minutes or so because, by then, his Lenster office would be shut and she would not be able to get his address or telephone number.

And even when she had got them both, she still held back. It was no part of her nature to interfere in the affairs of other people, but to her mind, her growing uneasiness was in the nature of a warning, and at last she rang Fergus up at his client's home in Manchester. It was some little time before she got in contact with him, but when she did, she could tell that he was quick to reflect her anxiety although he did his best to reassure her.

"Yes, Master Fergus," she said dutifully, and then, after a pause: "And when will you be home?"

"Tomorrow morning, in time for breakfast," he said promptly. "And look here, Maggie, if she gets in touch with you again, insist on knowing where she is — say I have told you to. Then ring me immediately."

"Yes, Master Fergus," she promised, not very hopefully. He had not heard Miss Vicky's voice —

"And in the meantime, 'phone the Ingletons. I don't know their number, but they live somewhere out Corby Chase way. Ask for Miss Glenda Ingleton. She used to be Vicky's best friend —"

He rang off and Maggie, putting on her steel-rimmed spectacles, hunted up the Ingleton's number. But Glenda was out, and it was only after a protracted argument with the butler that she obtained the telephone number of the house where she was visiting.

Another delay and then she was speaking to Glenda.

"No, I haven't seen Vicky for ages," she said, obviously more intrigued than alarmed at Maggie's question. "And what's more, there's everybody here that she used to know and they haven't said anything so — unless it is some new friend — Or perhaps she has eloped —" she finished hopefully and winced as Maggie banged the receiver down.

Almost immediately Fergus rang through again, and his first words were:

"I'm coming home immediately. Any news?"

Maggie repeated what she had just been told, and heard Fergus's heavy breathing over the telephone.

"I shall come home through Lenster — there is a call I must make. I shall be about two and a half hours — three, perhaps. Good-bye."

"Good-bye," Maggie said mechanically, and sat down to wait.

Thanking his stars that he had gone to Manchester by car and not by train, Fergus began his journey home. To his surprise, his elderly and touchy client had been singularly understanding and had insisted on his leaving then and there.

"For one thing, it's obvious that there is something wrong and your place is in your own home, and for another," she added caustically, "I can't see you giving my affairs the attention they merit with this on your mind! Off you go!"

And, thankfully, Fergus went. He drove mechanically, his mind full of this puzzle that Vicky had set him. Of course, there might not be a puzzle at all. Tomorrow, they might be laughing together at the whole thing. Yet he knew that he was afraid to the depths of his very being as he had never been afraid in his life before.

His call in Lenster was on Gil. Maggie, faithfully repeating every word that Glenda had said, had suggested elopement, and that had immediately recalled the young man to his mind. Fortunately he knew the boarding-house where Gil lived, but that did not help him much. Gil was out for the evening, and all that Fergus could do was to ask that he should get in touch with him immediately he returned.

His route home through Lenster took him past Sybil's shop and flat, and for a moment he hesitated. The flat was in darkness, but Sybil might have turned in early. She did sometimes after a heavy day. Should he knock her up and ask her if she knew anything about Vicky? But what could she know? Vicky had never discussed Sybil with him, but he had a pretty shrewd suspicion that the two girls had not really taken to one another. It was most unlikely that Sybil was the friend with whom Vicky was staying — and, in any case, if she had been, why should she not have told Maggie?

He went on his way, more and more convinced, as he got nearer home, that the solution of the mystery lay with Gil. If this idea needed confirmation, it seemed to Fergus that he had it when no message came through from Gil that night. And when, in the morning, the postman brought Vicky's letter, Fergus's face was grey and set.

His poor little Vicky! He had believed that he was doing his best for her in hurrying on the wedding. Their marriage would be founded on a basis of trust and, manlike, he believed that was enough to start on. In the future, he would teach her — but Vicky had felt no faith in the future as he had planned it. Doubtless she had met Pickard and had realised —

But where was she now? What had happened? Vicky might not love him, might never be his wife, but to Fergus she was the most precious thing in life and he was grimly determined to see that no harm befell her.

And the first thing he intended doing that morning was to go and see Gil and have it out with him —

And at half-past seven a rumpled and dressing-gown-clad Gil was staring at him in the drab hall of the boarding-house.

"But I didn't get your message," he protested. "Not that it would have made any difference if I had — no, wait a moment," as he saw the threat in Fergus's eyes. "What I mean is, I haven't a clue where Vicky is."

Fergus thrust Vicky's letter into his hand.

"Are you going to deny it — after this?"

Looking thoughtfully at Fergus, Gil took the letter and transferred his attention to it.

"Well?" Fergus said angrily. "Do you deny now that you saw her yesterday?"

"No," Gil said slowly. "I admit that. But —" he paused. "Imray, tell me, why are you so upset about this?"

"Good Lord, wouldn't anyone be?" Fergus exploded. "Vicky has vanished. Aren't you concerned about it?"

"Yes, I am," Gil admitted. "But then, you see, I happen to love her."

The eyes of the two men met, and in Gil's Fergus read a truth that he could not ignore. However much it appeared that facts contradicted Gil's statement, he did love Vicky. Fergus acknowledged it by giving a confidence in exchange.

"So do I," he said quietly.

Gil seized him by the arm.

"You do? Then what in the world is all this about? If you love Vicky and you've told her so —"

"But I haven't," Fergus admitted. "How could I? The child is in love with you! Even if she has not come to you, it is because she knows that she cares too much for you that she has gone away."

"This is crazy!" Gil said in exasperation. "Listen, you've got it the wrong way round! I tell you, I love her and what is more, she knows it! I proposed to her weeks ago and she turned me down! If she had suddenly realised that, after all, she did love me, she'd have come to me! But Vicky isn't the sort that changes her mind and, as it happens, she's in love with a blind fool who hasn't the sense to know it. You, man, you!"

"You're imagining things!" Fergus said harshly. "I should have known. Besides, this letter ——"

"What of it?" Gil asked. "You've got a past as well as Vicky, haven't you?"

"Not in that sense," Fergus retorted. "As far as I am concerned, there has never been any woman but Vicky!"

"Queer! Because Vicky told me, when we first met, that you were either engaged or about to be!"

"Vicky said that! But what nonsense! She must have misunderstood! In any case, who was it supposed to be?" Fergus demanded.

"Miss Allandyne," Gil said laconically.

Fergus was silent. Only he knew what had happened during that painful interview with Sybil when, for the first time, he had realised how different her reading of their friendship had been from his own, but now, as Gil spoke, the memory became not only painful but menacing.

"I told you I saw Vicky yesterday," Gil went on. "So I did. But I didn't speak to her. She was walking on the other side of the road and she was not alone. She was with Miss Allandyne. They were walking along Beauchamp Street and, as I watched, they turned down Gifford Street."

Towards Sybil's flat. There could be little doubt about it ——

"There's another thing," Gil said slowly. "That letter. Where did Vicky get the paper and envelope? If you go into a stationer's and buy an odd sheet of paper and envelope, it isn't that quality! Someone must have provided it for her."

Quickly Fergus took out his wallet. From it he took a sheet of paper on which Sybil had scribbled down the names of some books which, weeks ago, she had thought might interest his mother. It needed

177

no experienced detective to see that the two were identical.

"That appears to be that," Gil commented. "Oh, not the end of it, of course. But at least a definite beginning. She knows why Vicky ran away, and if I were you, I'd wring it out of her even if it means getting tough. I bet she knows where Vicky is, too!"

"Quite likely," Fergus agreed, carefully folding the two sheets of paper and putting them into his wallet. "Well, thanks, Pickard, for your help. I'll let you know what happens."

"I'd like to know," Gil admitted. "And if you want any help administering the third degree, just call on me!"

"I don't think that will be necessary," Fergus said grimly, and Gil did not hesitate to believe him.

Slowly Gil went upstairs, running his hand through his already tousled hair. Well, that was his good deed for the day!

"Fool that I am!" he soliloquised. "If I'd kept my big mouth shut, Vicky might have said 'yes' to me, one day!"

And he smiled, knowing that he could no more have stood in the way of Vicky and her real happiness than he could have flown.

There was no lack of genuineness about Sybil's surprise when she saw Fergus. And some alarm as well. Surely, in so short a time, he could not have found out anything that made him think she had been instrumental in getting rid of Vicky? Of course there was that letter — she did not know what Vicky had said, but she relied on the fact that Vicky had not wanted Fergus to follow her and was not likely to have said anything which would lead him straight to her.

Then a more flattering explanation of his presence so early occurred to her. It was not that he in any way associated her with what had happened, but that, in an emergency, it had seemed the most natural thing in the world to turn to her —

"Fergus!" she allowed a note of alarm to sound in her voice. That would be natural enough in the circumstances, even as Fergus knew them. "Is anything the matter?"

He looked at her silently, finding nothing but treachery in the inquiry and calculation in the eyes he had never realised before were so cold.

"What makes you think that there is?" he asked coolly.

Sybil felt her nerves tense. She laughed nervously.

"Well — it's rather an odd time for you to come and see me," she explained quickly. "And — you looked worried, Fergus!"

"I have every reason to be," he said quietly. "Vicky has run away without giving me any idea where she was going to."

"Fergus!" Her start of surprise would surely have convinced anyone. "But — why?"

"That is what I am wondering," Fergus admitted.

"But — hasn't she told you?" Sybil asked, sparring for time.

"No," Fergus said briefly.

"But she — surely she wrote —" Sybil corrected herself hastily.

"Oh, yes, she wrote to me." He took the note out of his pocket-book and handed it to her. "But, as you see, she gives me no real explanation."

Sybil glanced down at the note Vicky had written and felt a great wave of exultation and relief surge over her. Really, her luck was stupendous! First of all, Fergus had let her see this so that she knew exactly how much he knew and, secondly, Vicky could not have written anything more helpful to her own schemes.

She folded the sheet of paper and passed it back to him in silence.

"Well?" he demanded.

"I'm sorry, Fergus," she said with apparent reluctance. "But I think that explains everything!"

"Do you, indeed!" he retorted. "I'd like to know how you make that out!"

She hesitated and then, as if she had suddenly made up her mind to be frank, she said:

"Fergus, be honest. When Vicky promised to marry you, did you think that she loved you?"

"No," he said curtly.

Sybil shrugged her shoulders.

"Then don't you see, my dear?" she said gently. "Vicky has always been quite frank about her liking for that Pickard boy. But, on the other hand, he would not be able to provide her with the luxuries she has always been accustomed to for years — perhaps he never could. Whereas you —" she paused, but he motioned her to go on. "Fergus, I think, if you have any affection for Vicky, you should be glad about this," she said earnestly. "Isn't it obvious that she has met young Pickard and found that she cared too much for him to marry you for worldly considerations?"

"Is that what you think, Sybil?" he asked tonelessly, and Sybil laid her hand on his arm.

"I do, Fergus," she said gently.

"Then," he said harshly, "it will probably surprise you to know that Vicky has made no attempt to get into touch with Gil Pickard. You see, I know! I have just come straight from him!"

"Oh," Sybil caught her breath. "But — is he telling the truth? Mightn't they have decided that it would be best for her to keep out of your way for a bit? I mean, they might imagine you would try to stop them —"

"Why should I, since, according to what you told me the last time we met, I have no love for Vicky, only a mistaken sense of responsibility? Surely, in such circumstances, I ought to feel greatly relieved that someone else is responsible for her future!"

Sybil bit her lip. Fergus was being difficult — and obviously was suspicious of her. She regretted bitterly that she had ever spoken so frankly to him, but not for a moment was she going to let him realise how much at a disadvantage she felt.

"No man likes being made a fool of," she said

softly. "And your marriage has been announced very publicly, hasn't it?"

"So you really think she cares for young Pickard?" Fergus pondered.

"I do," she said firmly, and nearly screamed as Fergus suddenly laughed. It was a frightening laugh, not an expression of amusement but harsh, triumphant, merciless.

"Then how do you explain," he asked relentlessly, "that while, yesterday, Pickard had no communication whatever with Vicky, you and she were seen together?"

Of all the bad luck! Sybil's teeth grit together.

"Who says so?" she demanded loudly.

"Pickard," he admitted, perhaps a trifle unwillingly.

"Well, there you are, then!" Sybil said triumphantly.

"And this?" he indicated Vicky's letter that he still held in his hand.

"What of it?" she asked indifferently, and then, as he took another sheet of paper from his pocket and passed it to her she felt her cheeks blanch.

"I expect you recognise this, don't you? And, without much difficulty, you can see that the two sheets are identical, except for the fact that one is headed."

"Well?" Sybil asked brazenly.

Fergus hesitated. He had never been in love with Sybil, never thought of asking her to be his wife, but he had liked her and trusted her. She had come to be one of the family, and it was hateful now to know that she had returned the kindness and affection she had received with treachery and meanness.

"I'm sorry, Sybil," he said reluctantly. "But it isn't any good, you know! One coincidence, perhaps. But not more. You'd better tell me the truth now, because sooner or later I intend to get it — even if it means calling in the police! Vicky is a minor, you know!"

It was not his threat or the realisation that she had lost the game that made Sybil change her mind. Suddenly, it seemed to her that she had been a fool to lie to Fergus. She should have told him the truth, and, what was more, have made him realise that it was the truth!

"You're right, Fergus, I have lied," she admitted, her voice low and rich. "But — it was because Vicky asked me to! She wanted to be sure you would not know where she was! I wanted to tell you the truth, you see, but Vicky was afraid that you would not let her go — because of the money!"

"The money?" he said uncomprehendingly.

"The money your mother left her!" Sybil explained impatiently. "Vicky might marry you for the sake of security and comfort, Fergus, but it was a very different business when she realised —"

She paused, suddenly frightened at the expression on Fergus's face, and yet his voice was very quiet, almost gentle when he said:

"Just what did she realise, Sybil?"

"Why, how inconvenient it was for you to be denied the use of the capital that your mother's bequest has tied up," she explained hurriedly. "I think she realised how — beastly — the whole thing was and, perhaps, she felt ashamed of her own reason for promising to marry you. I can't tell you that! I only know that she begged me to help her get away — and I did."

"After having made it clear to her about this question of capital?" he asked. And she nodded.

"Of course!" Suddenly she clung to his arm, and if its rigidity made her realise how hopeless it was to go on, there was no suggestion of that in her eager voice: "Fergus, don't you understand how much you mean to me? Oh, I don't only mean what you are thinking! It is your integrity, your straightness that I am talking about now! I couldn't stand by and see you do a thing like this! I couldn't, Fergus!"

He stared at her in silence, and when at last he spoke, there was genuine amazement in his voice.

"You know, I believe you really think you mean that!" he said slowly.

"I do, I do!" she insisted.

"And you are convinced that you have discovered my reason for wanting to marry Vicky?" he went on quietly.

"Of course!" she said confidently. "What other

reason could it be? You have always said that she was a burden and responsibility —"

"Yes," he said heavily. "At first, I admit, that was what she seemed to me. And then, slowly, I began to realise that she was all the sunshine in life to me, my hope for the future. My little, little love!" The last words were almost a groan, and Sybil's hand dropped from his arm. She had fought against conviction, but now she knew that there was no more use in fighting. Incredible though it seemed, it was Vicky and not she whom Fergus loved.

And suddenly, she laughed as harshly and discordantly as Fergus himself had done not very long before.

"You'll have a job convincing Vicky of that!" she said viciously.

And then, to her surprise, Fergus smiled.

"No, my dear, thank heaven, I shall have no difficulty whatever in making her believe me! You see —"

And then he told her something so amazing that at first she could not believe he was telling her the truth.

But when, at last, conviction came, she collapsed, a weeping, broken woman, ready to tell Fergus everything he wanted to know.

CHAPTER THIRTEEN

FERGUS saw Vicky before she saw him. She was sitting tucked away in the corner of the big hotel lounge, a lonely, drooping little figure, shrinking away from all the other human beings who came and went about her.

Fergus did not try to steal up on her, but none the less, he had nearly reached her before, with a start, she was aware of his presence. She jumped to her feet and put out her hands defensively as if to keep him at a distance.

"You shouldn't have come!" she protested, and though her voice was low, he heard the note of sheer panic in it. She was terrified at the sight of him, and any compassion that Fergus might have felt for Sybil vanished from his heart at the sight of Vicky's fear. "You shouldn't have come — there was no need!"

"There was every need," Fergus said, and to Vicky his grim determination could mean only one thing.

She put her hands behind her back and lifted her head.

"I understand all about it," she said steadily. "And there is no need for you to marry me to get the money! You see, I am not going to accept the legacy — not a penny of it. So it will be quite all right for you!"

And, to her surprise, Fergus smiled. She could not know the relief and hope that went to make up that smile now that he knew Sybil had finally told him the truth and that this was the only barrier between them, but at least she knew it was not gratification at the thought of pecuniary gain that had prompted it.

Suddenly her composure crumpled.

"I don't understand," she faltered.

Fergus sat down on the couch and gently pulled her down beside him. Fortunately the big lounge was practically empty now and, in any case, a large and rather ugly palm made a useful barrier between them and the rest of the world.

"I want to tell you a story," he said gently. "Will you listen?"

She said nothing, because the touch of Fergus's hand, his nearness, seemed to have drained all the resistance from her. After a little pause, Fergus began to speak.

"A man and a girl were flung together very unceremoniously by fate. You would have said that they had nothing whatever in common — and perhaps they hadn't, to start with. And yet, right from the beginning, the man felt that she mattered — far more than was explained by the fact that she was a human being needing help. As a matter of fact, he was blind enough to think it was nothing more than that, and he resented the fact that it was impossible to avoid assuming what seemed a burden of responsibility that ought not to have fallen to him."

Vicky's lips parted, but if she had something to say, Fergus did not wait to hear what it was. He went on:

"Needless to say, the girl was not grateful for such grudging help —"

"I didn't want to accept anybody's help," Vicky interrupted. "I wouldn't have taken it from you, only — I had to. Besides, I saw you meant to get your money's worth!"

Fergus winced, but he made no comment. He could not blame Vicky for saying that, because it was only too true.

"I don't know exactly when things began to alter," he went on. "But — very soon, I think. And for the life of me, I could not understand why. You were rebellious and rude and as unresponsive as you could possibly be. And instead of wanting to give you a good spanking, as you richly deserved, I wanted, more than anything else in the world, to see you smile because you were happy!"

Vicky's heart turned over at the tenderness in his voice. And then she remembered. He was being very,

very clever, but — there was too much to be explained away. She must remember that and not let him take her in again.

"You showed it in a pretty queer way!" she said gruffly.

"Did you give me any choice?" he asked quickly. "When I found that, although you would accept gifts and entertainment from others — young Pickard, for instance — for me to offer you anything was to court instant refusal. Do you remember, the first time I paid you, I told you, quite honestly, that you were worth more than I had agreed to pay you? You practically flung the notes back in my face!"

"I didn't want your charity," Vicky muttered.

"I realised that," Fergus admitted. "And realised that it was largely my fault."

"Oh, no!" Vicky said quickly. "It was quite a lot me. I was resentful because you always seemed so — so maddeningly right about everything!"

"Did I, Vicky?" he smiled ruefully. "Now to me, it seems I made blunder after blunder!"

"No." She spoke so low that he had to bend nearer to hear what she was saying and, in spite of herself, her heart beat a little quicker. "You did your best to help me get things into proportion — neither refusing to face up to them nor dwelling too much on them."

"Thank you, Vicky, that's generous of you," he said softly. "All the same, I made mistakes — bad ones! A man does when he is jealous, you know!"

"Jealous?" her head lifted incredulously.

"Of Pickard. It seemed to me that I had every cause to be. You obviously enjoyed his company and you had much in common. He could make you laugh whereas I only hurt and angered you. Perhaps I've always taken life too seriously — it doesn't come easily to me to relax —"

"Your mother said you had never learned to play," Vicky said softly. "And that I had never learned to be serious. She told me that there was a lot we could teach one another."

His grip on her hand tightened and involuntarily Vicky's fingers curled a little round his.

"Thank you for telling me that, Vicky," he said gently. "I had meant to tell her — but somehow or other I never did. I'm glad she knew."

They were silent for a moment, and then Fergus went on:

"Like a fool, in my jealousy, I tried to keep you to myself, and of course you resented it. And there I was, completely helpless! The only thing I managed to do for you was to give you Larry — and I had to lie to do that!"

Vicky lifted her head and stared at him in bewilderment.

"Do you mean — are you trying to tell me that you loved me?" she asked. "Oh, but you couldn't have done —"

"I loved you — but not enough," he told her gravely. "That came later. If you want to know exactly when, it was the night of the Hospital Ball. I held you in my arms — and then, later, I bathed your poor little foot — I very nearly kissed it, only I was afraid to because I knew you would fly out of my house like a frightened bird if I did. And I had learned by then that nothing mattered except your safety, your happiness — even at the cost of my own. Vicky —" His arm slipped round her shoulders and she heard the vibrant note of passion, muted though it was, in his voice. "Tell me you believe me! Tell me that it matters to you!"

Here, in the shelter of his arms, she could shut her ears to the memory of Sybil's story, she could defy her doubts — certainties — that nothing but money was of any importance to him. Perhaps it was folly, but Vicky, in that supreme minute, listened to her heart and not her head. And her heart told her to trust him, to give her chance of happiness into his keeping, no matter what the risk —

"I knew that night, too," she said, low-voiced. "I did not know that you loved me, but — I knew that

187

you were different. It was as if I recognised you for the first time."

Fergus's arm tightened round her shoulders.

"You're going to marry me — as soon as possible," he said masterfully.

"Yes," Vicky promised softly.

His voice, caressing and deeply moved, was soft in her ear.

"All my life I'm going to remember this minute — remember that you've trusted me when, heaven knows, you've little cause to! And we have the rest of our lives for me to prove to you that you haven't made a mistake. All the same, I want you to know the whole story. Then I shall know you are safe for always from people like — Sybil —"

He saw the stab of fear in her grey eyes and went on quickly:

"I told you I wanted your happiness more than anything — and I thought you would find it with Pickard. Only he still has his way to make, so —" He drew a deep breath. "Darling, my mother left you nothing. But — I had to look after you, and it was the only way. You would not have taken anything from me, so —"

"Fergus!" She drew back from him to search his face. "You mean — *you* did that — for me!"

"I love you," he said simply.

He did! He must do! Nothing but love could have prompted such a gesture. Like Fergus, she would be glad all her life that she had trusted him without proof. Yet she knew that what he had just told her was of infinite value to her. It was as if a clear, unwavering light had dismissed all the shadows, real and imaginary, from her heart. And it was a light that would never fail. She could face the future unafraid.

"I love you, Fergus," she whispered, her heart in her eyes.

An elderly visitor, intent on writing a letter, came to a desk nearby. He gave a grunt that might have expressed annoyance or sympathy and turned away. But he need not have worried. Vicky and Fergus were in a world of their own and had not even seen him!

Each month from Harlequin

8 NEW FULL LENGTH ROMANCE NOVELS

Here are some recent titles:

FREE!!!
Did you know......?

that just by mailing in the coupon below you can receive a brand new, up-to-date "Harlequin Romance Catalogue" listing literally hundreds of Harlequin Romances you probably thought were out of print.

Now you can shop in your own home for novels by your favorite Harlequin authors — the Essie Summers you wanted to read, the Violet Winspear you missed, the Mary Burchell you thought wasn't available anymore!

They're all listed in the "Harlequin Romance Catalogue". And something else too — the books are listed in numerical sequence, — so you can fill in the missing numbers in your library.

Don't delay — mail the coupon below to us today. We'll promptly send you the "Harlequin Romance Catalogue"

PLEASE NOTE: Harlequin Romance Catalogue of available titles is revised every three months.

FREE!

Have You Missed Any of These

Harlequin Romances?

ZZ